MW00794968

Killer Cruise

Dawn Brookes

Large Print Edition

Killer
Cruise

A Rachel Prince Mystery

Dawn Brookes

Oakwood Publishing

Paperback Edition 2019

Large Print 2019

Kindle Edition 2019

Large Print ISBN: 978-1-913065-01-0

Copyright © DAWN BROOKES 2019

Cover Design: Janet Dado

To Sue
BFF

Chapter 1

As Rachel gazed up out of the rear window of the old Bentley, the glow from the sun appeared to be caressing the magnificent *Coral Queen*. The *Coral* had become a ship she was extremely fond of, in spite of a few minor hiccups from puzzling murder conundrums on the two cruise holidays she'd previously spent on board.

"Almost there, ladies." Marjorie's chauffeur broke the amicable silence in the rear of the car. Rachel was spending a fortnight accompanying her eighty-six-year-old friend, Lady Marjorie Snellthorpe, whom she'd met under stressful circumstances on her very first cruise. Afterwards they had become firm friends and Rachel had grown increasingly fond of the stoical older woman.

"Thank you, Johnson, my old bones were beginning to stiffen up. Are you alright, dear?" Marjorie smiled at Rachel.

"I'm great, thanks. I was just admiring the *Coral,* she's berthed over there."

"She is rather wonderful, isn't she?" replied Marjorie as they continued the drive towards the port's entrance. A few minutes later they were parked up at a drop-off area in front of the passenger terminal. Johnson leapt out of the car with surprising agility for someone much older than Rachel and opened the door for Lady Marjorie before moving round to let Rachel out.

He opened the boot, which had required packing with great precision due to its size, and the ship's crew were soon attending to their luggage. Johnson insisted on carrying the hand luggage for both of them, despite protests from Rachel, reminding her how she felt part of a bygone era whenever she was with Marjorie. Growing up in a vicarage, she was used to helping other people rather than being helped herself and being pampered didn't come naturally.

Her father, vicar of St Crispin's in the village of Brodthorpe, Hertfordshire, always set a perfect example of the 'give and you shall receive' philosophy. The only assistance the family had ever had came from a cook hired to help her mother during Rachel's early childhood. Rachel's mother was the perfect hostess and for the most part played the role of the vicar's wife well, with just the occasional rebellion. One such mutiny had occurred the previous week when Rachel was visiting for the weekend.

"I draw the line at overnighters with Girl Guides in the church, Brendan. It's just not going to happen."

"The overnighter or you being one of the responsible adults?" Her father had laughed.

"You know full well what I mean. I'm not cooking, baking, cosseting or babysitting a group of giggly girls. I'm very sorry Clara's ill, but my sympathy does not stretch to replacing all and sundry every time something goes wrong. I already have the village fête, the women's institute and your AGM to cater for this weekend, and now you're asking me to feed fifteen girls for two days and sleep – or not – in the church with them! No, Brendan. Enough is enough. Find someone else or cancel it, I don't care which."

Brendan Prince knew when he was beaten. He hugged his wife and conceded, looking pleadingly towards Rachel who'd agreed to step into the breach, and as it happened, had had enormous fun. Her mother had softened enough to supply meals while Rachel baked enough cakes to feed all of the Girl Guide troops for miles around.

Rachel stretched her legs after getting out of the car and ran up and down on the spot for a few minutes to shake away the effects of the relatively short car journey. She had already jogged around Hyde Park first thing, knowing that the day would be sedentary and not wanting to miss out on her daily exercise. No-one in the family understood where her fitness-fanatic behaviour came from except herself. The running bug she'd picked up at university when she'd found herself homesick and after feeling confined during the first year living in halls of residence. It became more of an obsession during her first year of police training when she'd failed to run down a youth who had knocked an elderly woman to the ground and snatched her handbag. Her colleague had stopped to give support to the woman and Rachel had given chase, but the youth had lost her after running up a hill with comparative ease and leaping over a wall. Disgusted with her apparent lack of fitness, she'd trained harder and harder and prided herself on never failing to run anyone down since.

Marjorie and Johnson waited patiently for her to finish jogging on the spot and retrieve her handbag from the car.

"Ready?" the old lady asked.

"Ready," replied Rachel, noticing the enthusiastic crowds building up both inside and outside the terminal.

As VIP passengers, courtesy of Marjorie's multiple cruises, which had more recently been extended to free cruises for life, they would not have to wait in the orderly snake-like queue forming in the terminal. Marjorie took Rachel's arm and they walked towards the entrance for platinum passengers. The staff welcomed them and asked if they needed assistance with their bags, which Rachel declined quickly, claiming them from Johnson before he could object.

"Goodbye, Johnson. Safe journey home, and enjoy your holiday," Marjorie intervened to prevent a scene.

"Thank you, My Lady, I will." He tipped his cap and waved until they'd passed through the passenger entrance towards security. Marjorie was offered wheelchair assistance for the long trek up to the ship's passenger entrance, which she graciously accepted. Rachel put one bag on her shoulder and extended the handle of Marjorie's hand luggage to drag it along behind her.

"Where's Johnson going for his holiday?"

"Where he goes every year – fishing in the Scottish Highlands. He loves it up there, walks for miles after spending hours on end ogling the water for signs of a catch."

"That explains why he's so agile," remarked Rachel.

"He's a keen fisherman," Marjorie continued. "I think that's the reason Ralph chose him as our chauffeur – it was something my late husband loved to do too. So the two of them would up-sticks and spend days sitting in front of some river, loch or anything else they could fish in."

"Sounds like it's not your thing."

"You're absolutely right, my dear. It's one pastime I've never been able to comprehend. Dreadfully dull, but each to their own, as they say. I never told Ralph, but I don't think it's fair to catch fish with a hook only to throw them back in the water again. Although to be fair, he did sometimes eat what he caught."

After slowly making their way up the makeshift ramp, not because the volunteer pushing Marjorie's wheelchair was slow, but because people joining the ship ahead of them were taking their time, they finally arrived on board where Marjorie insisted she could walk.

"I'll be alright now, thank you. I'm fine on the flat, really."

"Okay, Madam." The jolly volunteer made his way back with the empty wheelchair to assist with the next passenger needing help, but not before Marjorie had given him a generous tip for his kindness.

The initial impression on entering the grand atrium never failed to take Rachel's breath away. She couldn't help admiring the thick, shiny marble pillars, polished brass stair rails and the immaculate cleanliness.

Marjorie looked tired. "Shall we sit for a while?" asked Rachel, to which the old lady nodded. They found seats at a small table away from where the passengers were boarding. The surrounding tables were already filling up as some people had the same idea. Others were wandering around admiring the opulence of the atrium, which spanned two decks and formed the main hub of activity and the retail section of the vessel. A waiter who had been about to offer them champagne on boarding until he'd noticed Rachel's hands were full brought them complementary flutes to have while they sat.

"I do hope there's a crime on board so that we can do a bit of detecting," said Marjorie gleefully.

"And I do hope there isn't," replied Rachel, laughing.

Chapter 2

"Come on, Sarah, questionnaire time," called Brigitte.

Sarah looked up at her French colleague from where she'd been lounging after checking through new passenger records and pondering over who might need medical attention. Groaning, she hauled herself from the comfortable sofa in Senior Nurse Gwen Sumner's office. Gwen herself had taken the day off and joined back-to-back passengers on a coach tour to London.

"I love turnaround days and meeting new passengers, but honestly, Brigitte – if we have another cruise like the last, I'm out of here." Sarah had worked as a nurse for Queen Cruises for almost two years and considered herself fortunate that she'd only worked on the one ship so far.

A ship that also happens to be the largest in the fleet.

She smiled. The transatlantic crossing they had just returned from had resulted in the medical centre being inundated from day one. The return crossing was rough and passengers had struggled with the conditions, either falling down or throwing up all over the ship. In addition to that, the crew had been particularly accident prone, injuring themselves on a daily basis. Most of the injuries occurred when crew became unable to maintain their footing while rushing around attending to passengers.

"Be thankful it wasn't worse," said Brigitte.

"It was bad enough – I would say we're due a quiet spell, but Rachel and Marjorie are joining us today and you know what that means!"

"Noooo, it's not going to happen. Third time lucky – no murders this voyage, not even a hint of murder." Brigitte had missed the previous cruise Rachel had taken after her father had been involved in a car accident.

"Let's hope not. Anyway, I'm ready. Where's Bernard?"

"I don't know – he said he was going to enjoy his day off and sleep all day before surgery tonight."

Sarah sighed. The medical centre held two walk-in surgeries each day, and staff also attended emergencies night and day. The nurses and doctors took turns being on call, with the nurses usually triaging patients that might need to be seen by a doctor, treating many themselves. As a rule, Dr Graham Bentley, the chief medical officer, treated passengers while Alex Romano, the junior doctor or baby doc as he was affectionately referred to, managed the health of the crew.

"Did Alex do the London trip?"

"No, he said he was going to Portsmouth to visit the *Victory* or something. Whatever that is?"

"HMS *Victory*, it's an old gunship. I'm surprised you haven't heard of it as it played a major part in the Battle of Trafalgar during the Napoleonic Wars. I think we beat your lot, along with the Spanish."

"Pah, I never was interested in history, and least of all in war history. There's enough going on in the world today without harking back to the past."

"If only we would learn from history," Sarah muttered as they made their way off the ship to the passenger terminal.

"Those lads are going to be trouble," said Sarah as they made their way back on board after checking through passenger health questionnaires. A group of thirty young men aged between twenty-one and twenty-three were taking the cruise as a stag party. Sarah noticed the already boisterous and rowdy group causing consternation among some of the older passengers, while others looked less than patient, raising their eyebrows and rolling their eyes.

"I think you're right, they will be, but hopefully for security, not for us," answered Brigitte.

"Poor Waverley, he's already dreading this cruise with Rachel joining us. I do think his hands are going to be full keeping that lot under control."

"Not to mention them." Brigitte nodded towards an American all-girl group, similar ages to the boys.

"Mm, could be a satisfying blend or a toxic combination, a bit like Bernard's cocktails."

"Don't talk to me about Bernard or his cocktails."

Brigitte and Bernard had developed a good friendship, but it could be volatile at times due to their opposite personalities. Bernard, a nurse from the Philippines, could be a tease, while Brigitte was more serious and often spoke her mind before engaging her brain. It sometimes resulted in heated debate, but Sarah was thankful that underneath it all, they liked each other, and when push came to shove, they had each other's backs.

"He does like to experiment," Sarah laughed. "The only successful secret cocktail recipe he has produced is the Stinger – not that I like them. They are like Marmite: you love them or you hate them."

"They're alright I suppose, but I prefer wine, being French."

"Anyway, I'm going to track down Rachel and Lady Snellthorpe before dinner and evening surgery. See you later." Sarah tapped her friend and colleague on the shoulder and headed towards the main atrium.

She spotted Lady Marjorie's unmistakable head of bright white hair, immaculately permed, before seeing Rachel partially hidden by a pillar. She sneaked up behind her, holding her finger to her lips to alert Marjorie not to give the game away, and grabbed her shoulders from behind. Rachel calmly got up from her chair before hugging Sarah excitedly. They had been best friends since school.

"Why weren't you surprised?" Sarah felt disappointed.

"I saw you coming through the glass. If you want to surprise people, you're going to have to tell the staff not to do such a good job of the cleaning."

Rachel laughed as Sarah looked at the gleaming glass balustrade next to the table and realised what she meant – her reflection was clearly visible, not only in the glass, but also the table and the marble pillars.

"Hello, Lady Snellthorpe. It's lovely to see you again." Sarah hugged the old lady who had stood to greet her.

"Bah, you can do away with the Lady Snellthorpe business. Marjorie to you, and I'll brook no argument. You look lovely in that pristine white uniform, my dear, and it's a pleasure to see you again."

"Thank you," answered Sarah, standing back and studying the elderly lady. A spritely woman for her age, and immaculately dressed and manicured as usual. She recognised the sky-blue Ralph Lauren suit and the Armani blouse immediately. "You don't look so bad yourself. Are you keeping well, Marjorie?"

"Quite well, thank you."

Sarah joined them at the table and gratefully accepted a glass of orange juice from one of the waiters. Marjorie was unlikely to say even if she weren't well, a proud woman who believed in the stiff upper lip mentality that many people her age adhered to.

"How was the New York trip?" asked Rachel.

"New York was fine – no murder en route, unlike when you were with us, but the return sailing was rough the first few days. Lots of passengers were seasick. We haven't had much time to catch our breath, but this journey looks good. The forecast is favourable, and the multiple stops should keep people entertained, allowing the crew to get their land legs back again as we all get more shore leave."

An announcement came over the ship's loudspeakers informing them of a compulsory safety drill before dinner.

"I'd better go and drop this hand luggage off in our rooms," said Rachel. "I'll meet you at our Muster Station, Marjorie.

"Yes, I need to change uniforms quickly. One of the passengers spilt tea downstairs and my skirt was splashed."

"Barely noticeable," remarked Marjorie.

"I know, but better to give a good impression to passengers on their first day," answered Sarah, winking. She hugged Rachel and Marjorie again before leaving. "I can't wait to introduce you to Jason."

"We can't wait either, can we, Marjorie?"

"We are very much looking forward to it," answered Marjorie.

"I'll let you know when I can arrange it. Catch you later."

Sarah bounced away happily. She was indeed looking forward to introducing her new boyfriend Jason to Rachel. A best friend's appraisal was always welcome.

Chapter 3

The next evening, Rachel couldn't help but notice the brash Freddie Mercury lookalike making his way towards her. He'd been doing the rounds in the bar where she and Marjorie were having a quiet after-dinner cocktail.

"Oh dear. Here comes trouble," remarked Marjorie.

"Allo, darling." The stench of alcohol-fuelled breath almost knocked her out as the man sat on the bar stool next to Rachel. Around six-foot tall, with short dyed black hair, black moustache and large, prominent front teeth, he was already worse for wear. At eight o'clock in the evening, the night was yet young. He spoke with a cockney accent and his lecherous blood-shot green eyes told Rachel all she needed to know about him.

"How do you do?" Marjorie tried to intervene on her behalf. Rachel was used to unwanted attention, being tall with blonde hair, blue eyes, and told by so many how beautiful she looked. Being so attractive wasn't always a positive thing, but she could handle it. This man had already caused quite a commotion in the bar, a number of men standing up and threatening him, and the policewoman in Rachel had been inadvertently observing his behaviour since he came in. Almost as soon as he'd entered, he'd argued with a man in a suit. The man had grabbed his arm in an attempt to lead him out, but 'Freddie Mercury' had pushed him away, causing the man to shrug his shoulders and leave.

The man before her now was wearing a white Elvis Presley style jumpsuit decorated with ribbons and sequins. Not the normal white vest and trousers she remembered from seeing pictures of Freddie Mercury, if that was who he was imitating. He also wore smudged bright red lipstick, eyeliner and thick mascara – he had to be a member of the on-board entertainment. She got another whiff of alcohol mixed with cigarette smoke on his breath as he leaned closer, blocking Marjorie.

"I was talking to 'er, Grandma." His speech was slurred and he almost fell over as he grabbed Rachel's wrist. Rachel wanted to give him a swift karate chop for his rudeness to her elderly friend, but she made allowances for the fact he was in a drunken stupor.

"Sir, I respectfully suggest it might be better if you went elsewhere. I'm having a drink with my friend. Please take your hand off me." Rachel warned him, forcing herself to be as pleasant as she could muster.

"Oh, come on, give a geezer a break. You looking for a good time?" His grip grew tighter and he pulled her closer. Looking down at her wrist, Rachel noticed a red mark extending beyond where his hand was holding her tight. It was becoming painful.

"I am having a good time, thank you. Now, you're hurting me, so for the last time, please remove your hand."

"Or what?" he spluttered, spraying saliva over her dress. Rachel had had enough. Moving as quickly and stealthily as a panther, she grabbed his hand and twisted his arm behind his back in an instant, gritting her teeth.

"Or this—"

He cried out, drawing even more attention to the scene. Heads were turning all around.

"Alright, let go o' me."

Rachel noticed a large man getting up from another stool, looking angry. She released Freddie's arm as a security guard entered the bar and approached him.

"Mr Mercury, sir, I'm going to have to ask you to come with me."

Rachel gawped. "Really?"

The guard rolled his eyes and mouthed, "I know, it's what he likes to be called!"

The man tried to straighten himself and square up to the security guard, but his effort was a pathetic attempt, and he was no match for the strapping six-foot-three guard, whose name badge revealed him as Jason Goodridge. Rachel knew at once that he was a recent addition to the security team working on board the *Coral Queen*, and more importantly, he was Sarah's new boyfriend.

Mercury conceded defeat and allowed Jason to lead him out of the bar.

"Well, cruising has certainly been more interesting since I met you, Rachel Prince," chuckled Marjorie, eyes twinkling.

"It can be entertaining at times, although deadly and extremely annoying at others," Rachel retorted, mulling over her previous cruises tracking down murderers. It was fun travelling with Marjorie, who had asked Rachel to accompany her on this cruise around the Baltic Sea as she no longer enjoyed travelling alone and her son despised cruising. Rachel was only too pleased to oblige and they were happily ensconced in luxury suites at the back of deck fifteen with a butler shared between them. Marjorie insisted on paying for Rachel who had reluctantly accepted, knowing that once the old lady's mind was made up, there was no changing it.

"Do you suppose that was his real name?" asked Rachel.

"No, I don't think so. He looks like he might be one of the entertainers; I read in the *Coral News* there was a Queen tribute act on board. He may be a fanatic, or worse still, a member of the band, I suppose."

"Let's hope he's not one of the band or they will be one short – I can't see him sobering up anytime soon. Are they playing tonight?"

"I believe so, but I didn't notice where or when. Not my thing, I prefer heavy metal." Marjorie giggled again, causing Rachel to join in.

"Yeah, right!"

"You handled yourself well there, ma'am." A pleasant American voice interrupted their conversation. Rachel looked down from her bar stool to see a short, stocky man in his sixties with silver-grey hair and a snow-white moustache, similar to Marjorie's hair colour. He continued in his southern drawl, "He was getting on my last nerve." The man giggled at his own joke. "The wife told me to come to your aid, but you moved pretty quickly before I got the chance. I don't move as fast as I used to. May I buy you both a drink and would you like to join Mabel and me?" He pointed towards a table for four where an elegant bleached-blonde lady, wearing an emerald green dress, was waving. Rachel looked at Marjorie to check.

"Thank you. That would be most kind," the old lady answered. "I'll have another one of these splendid cocktails please."

Rachel smiled at the man and answered, "The same – if you're sure that's alright?"

"It would be my pleasure." He turned to a barman and ordered the drinks.

They made their way over to the table where Mabel was sitting.

"Howdy." The woman spoke in a high-pitched voice. "I haven't seen moves like that in a long time. Where d'you learn to do that?"

Rachel, always reluctant to divulge the fact she worked as a policewoman, answered honestly, "Karate black belt. I like to practise now and then."

"Well, he's lucky he didn't get the chop then, eh, Mabel?" The man laughed again as he arrived with two Blue Lagoons. "I'm Ron, by the way, and this is my wife, Mabel."

"I'm Rachel."

"And I'm Marjorie," said Marjorie with the twinkle that hadn't left her eye. It was obvious she was enjoying herself.

"That's a mighty fine upper-crust English accent you have there, Marjorie," said Ron, good-naturedly. "Are you two related?"

"No," answered Marjorie. "But I have come to view Rachel as a granddaughter over the past few years. She's become part of the family," she said affectionately.

Rachel smiled at the unexpected compliment and had to agree that she and Marjorie had become very close in recent months. Rachel had taken a job in the police force in north London, and knowing how expensive London was to live in, Marjorie had offered her a flat she owned in the West End at a much reduced rent. Rachel had been reluctant to accept the offer, but Marjorie had insisted.

"It's an apartment that was used by my husband for international visitors when he ran the business. Since Ralph died, it sits empty as Jeremy puts overseas people up at his home now. Gives him the opportunity to show off. I was mulling over the idea of selling the place so you would be doing me a huge favour occupying it. Save me the bother."

Rachel finally accepted, and despite a few guilt pangs, couldn't be happier with her new apartment just a short distance from Harrods in Knightsbridge.

Ron and Mabel turned out to be pleasant company. They explained they were from Texas with Ron owning a cattle ranch inherited from his grandparents.

"Daddy didn't want anything to do with it. Couldn't wait to escape, but I love it out there, solitary and wild. I would have given it all up for Mabel, though. She was born and bred in the city, but fell in love with me and the ranch in that order." He squeezed his wife's hand. "We're getting too old for all the work involved now; we haven't been blessed with children, so it looks like we might have to sell up the old place soon." He looked momentarily saddened by this proclamation, and Mabel squeezed his hand back. "But I have a great neighbour and his son who will buy us out whenever we're ready. We'll be able to live in the house for as long as we like, though."

"That guy who was bothering you ladies is lead singer in a Queen tribute band, you know. Only saw them perform last night and he was brilliant, although a bit too risqué for our liking," said Mabel.

"Oh really? They're supposed to be performing tonight, too," remarked Marjorie.

"Is that so?" Mabel pulled a copy of the *Coral News*, a daily brochure listing all activities and events available on board ship, from her bag. "Oh, so they are, eleven o'clock in the Culture Lounge. Let's hope there are two lead singers."

"Too late for me, I'm afraid," said Marjorie. "Otherwise I'd be tempted to see if he's sobered up by then. What about you, Rachel?"

"I just might go out of curiosity, if Sarah's up for it."

"Who's Sarah?" asked Mabel.

"She's my best friend who works on board as a ship's nurse. We're meeting up once she's finished work for the evening. Here she comes now."

Sarah walked in, looking dazzling as usual in her pristine white officer's uniform, compulsory attire in the passenger areas. She hugged Rachel and kissed Marjorie on the cheek.

"Hello, you two." She looked at Ron and Mabel. "Good evening, sir, madam."

Rachel introduced the couple and Sarah joined them. Ron enjoyed relating the story of Rachel's lightning moves fending off the troublesome entertainer, ending with the fact the man was supposed to be performing later in the evening.

"I can tell you want to go," said Sarah, laughing at Rachel's eager face. "I have heard about the band. They've joined us on a three month contract." Sarah sounded like they had already made an impression, but didn't elaborate.

Rachel nodded and the matter was settled.

"Can I get you a drink?" Ron offered.

"No, you cannot," interjected Marjorie. "It's my turn, but might I ask you to do the honours, Rachel? Here's my card."

After buying a round of drinks, Rachel sat down and told Sarah how they had inadvertently met Jason who had been the man of the moment, escorting Mr Freddie Mercury out of the bar following the unwelcome incident. Sarah blushed at the mention of Jason's name. Rachel was happy for her.

"We didn't get the opportunity to introduce ourselves, though."

"Freddie Mercury can't be his real name, can it?" asked Marjorie.

"No, it's not," Sarah replied. "His name is Dominic, Dominic Venables, but he will only answer to Dom – or Freddie. He is apparently going to change his name by deed poll soon, though, according to the drummer."

"My, my!" exclaimed Ron. "As long as we don't meet an Elvis Presley or Dolly Parton – not that I'd complain about the latter – on board ship, or I'll start thinking I'm ready for a rest home." They all laughed, good naturedly.

After finishing her drink, Marjorie stood up. "If you young things don't mind, it's time for me to retire."

"I'll walk you," Rachel offered.

"No need, dear. I'm going to take a stroll on the upper decks first."

Rachel knew that Marjorie and her late husband had always strolled around the open decks before going to bed, something Marjorie chose to do alone as she said it helped her feel close to him.

"Time for us to go too," declared Mabel. "I've got an appointment for a manicure early tomorrow morning."

Left alone, Rachel asked Sarah how her day had been.

"Relatively quiet – a healthy group of passengers so far. Day two and no murders – that's got to be a bonus."

"If you count boarding day as day one, then yes, so far, so good."

The cacophonous din of rock music blaring from the Culture Lounge greeted them.

"I've never been here before," said Rachel. "There's still so much to explore on board."

The band was warming up. The lounge was already full and the two friends struggled to find anywhere to sit. The cavernous room resembled a disco in many ways with a dance floor in front of the stage where the band was tuning instruments. The lighting was dim around the tables with kaleidoscopic rotating lamps flashing towards the dance floor and the stage.

"No sign of Freddie," said Rachel as they perched themselves on two bar stools on the edge of a large table.

"Gordon doesn't look happy," Sarah remarked.

"Who's Gordon?"

"Gordon Venables. He's the new cruise director, taken over from Matt who decided to join the Caribbean route."

Rachel saw a small, slim man with dark-brown hair, dressed in a navy-blue suit, frantically speaking into his radio just off the side of the stage. The other members of the band continued testing their instruments and microphones at mega-too-loud decibels. Rachel could barely hear Sarah, they were shouting above the thunderous sound of the bass.

"He does look stressed, poor man."

It was quarter past eleven and the crowd was becoming more boisterous and fractious by the minute. Gordon walked towards the main microphone.

"Apologies, ladies and gentlemen, there will be a short delay while we wait for our lead singer—"

"Boo, boo, boo!" the crowd yelled, drowning out the dulcet tones of the cruise director.

"Oh dear," said Sarah. "He's really not having a good day – one of the dancers in the early evening theatre show sprained her ankle and had to pull out of the second show, and now this."

"How do you know all this?"

"I was called over to the theatre to treat the sprain."

As if by magic, the lights dimmed, the band struck up a rousing intro and Freddie-cum-Dom paraded on stage, belting out a rendition of *Killer Queen*. It did the trick. His jumping and gyrating with the microphone attached to a mobile stand whipped the mainly middle-aged and largely inebriated crowd into a state of frenzy. A good performer, Rachel had to admit.

"The cynic in me says that was staged," she shouted above the noise.

Sarah was shaking her head, bemused and looking as confused as Rachel. The atmosphere was rocking with sound vibrations they could actually feel underneath their feet following the increase in volume. The sudden appearance of the elusive Freddie had caused the crowd to go into a feverish euphoria. Gordon ran off stage, wiping sweat from his forehead with a handkerchief.

Rachel watched the theatrical Freddie, mesmerised by his mannerisms. "I can imagine him practising in his bedroom, performing to old videos to be as good as this. Queen was before my time, but he seems about right. They certainly don't use mics like that anymore, as far as I'm aware."

"Thankfully. He's obviously an obsessed eccentric, but a brilliant performer," Sarah shouted back. "As long as he keeps the passengers happy, although I fear the band might end up being more trouble than it's worth."

An hour later, while the band left the stage for a break, Rachel and Sarah enjoyed the relative quiet.

"Do you mind if we call it a night? I'm on call in the morning," said Sarah.

"Yes, that's fine with me. They are a good group, I'll give them that – shame Mr Mercury doesn't behave a bit better when not on stage."

While waiting for Sarah to come out of the ladies, Rachel saw Dom-cum-Freddie standing in the corridor, yelling at another man. The lead guitarist she suspected, although she wasn't certain.

"If you think you're ever gonna be good enough to take over from me – forget it! Don't think I don't know what's going on behind my back. You're not good enough! You'll never be good enough."

Following this diatribe, Freddie barged past Rachel, knocking her left shoulder as he did so. The man who had been shouted at was too busy licking his wounds to see her either and he sulkily followed Freddie back towards the stage.

Sarah returned.

"He might be a good singer, but he's a real pain in the backside." Rachel glared after both men.

"What happened?"

"Mr blooming egocentric dinosaur barged into me after giving one of his band mates a tongue lashing. He really needs to learn some manners."

"Oh dear, I'm sorry. Don't worry, Rachel, I suspect he won't last long on board the *Coral Queen* if he starts annoying the passengers like that."

"I won't be complaining, but it will not be long before someone else does, I'm afraid. Anyway, no harm done, but someone might just lash out at him if he's not careful."

They parted company at the lifts and Rachel made her way up to deck fifteen and her luxury suite, *Killer Queen* still buzzing around in her head.

Chapter 4

The following morning, Rachel joined Marjorie for breakfast in her suite after going for a run around deck sixteen. Mario, their butler from El Salvador who she knew from previous voyages, brought in extra coffee on seeing Rachel.

"I knew you would want coffee, ma'am Rachel, so I took liberty of ordering extra."

"Thanks, Mario. I must be taking too many cruise holidays if you know me that well!"

"Not nearly enough, ma'am." He placed the tray on a table and left them to it.

They sat out on the large balcony facing the expansive sea behind the ship as their suites were situated, one either side, at the rear of deck fifteen. Today there was no sea view as they were docked in Copenhagen harbour. Rachel poured them both coffee and took in deep breaths of salt-filled air.

"Did you enjoy your evening last night?" asked Marjorie.

"It was incredibly noisy, but the tribute band was surprisingly good. My father was a fan of Queen in their early days so I'm familiar with some of their music. He keeps it secret from his parishioners, though."

"I don't see why. I am pleased I didn't come, though; I'm not a fan of loud pop music. Give me Brahms any day of the week. So the rather rude Dominic Venables managed to sober up in time, did he?"

"I couldn't swear to him being sober, but he did deign to turn up, fifteen minutes late, just as the crowd was getting agitated about the wait. It could have been a ploy for all I know, although the new cruise director looked stressed out of his head. Sarah said he'd had a bad first sea day. Anyway, that's enough about the obnoxious Dom if you don't mind? What would you like to do today, Marjorie?"

"Nothing too strenuous, if that's alright? Perhaps a look at the Little Mermaid as she's not long returned from touring the globe, I understand, and then changing of the guard at the palace. I'm happy to take a taxi if you want to do something more exciting, though."

"Nope, that sounds very good to me. I had quite a late night."

Rachel took a quick shower after breakfast and dressed in cropped denim jeans, a faded jade t-shirt and a pair of white Doc Martin sandals. Marjorie looked quintessentially British in a dark-blue summer skirt and jacket with a pair of fitted beige open-toed shoes and handbag to match. The cotton floral print blouse with colours that enhanced her outfit finished it off to a tee. Rachel admired her friend's dress sense. Marjorie always took time over her appearance and rarely had a hair out of place. Her white hair, recently permed, accentuated her almost regal demeanour. *She could have been a duchess as well as a lady.*

"I feel positively underdressed," she said forlornly.

"You look beautiful, my dear, as you always do."

"Not as glamorous as you, but it's too late for me to change now anyway."

Rachel took the old lady's arm and they headed towards the central lifts and down to deck three where they could leave the ship via security and makeshift steps. The ship's photographers were strategically positioned on the dockside, offering to take photos before passengers left for their outings. The happy duo obliged, before ambling along towards the building that formed the port's customs.

Just before they entered through a pair of open doors, the noise of someone gasping behind her caused Rachel to swing round. Following the gasping woman's gaze, she looked on in horror as a body hurtled downwards, towards the sea from somewhere near the top of the ship. A few other passengers had turned around too, and soon afterwards there was a loud splash.

Pandemonium followed and one of the passengers screamed. A life buoy was thrown into the water from one of the lower decks and the man overboard siren sounded. Two officers and a dock worker dived into the black water.

"Ladies and gentlemen, please move along." An officer quickly took charge and directed passengers away from the scene, while others screened off the area. Marjorie looked at Rachel.

"Was that who I think it was?"

"It certainly looked like it, but I didn't get a good enough look. It all happened so quickly. The jumpsuit looked about right, though."

They were hurriedly escorted towards the exit and, accepting there was nothing they could do, they complied, agreeing to continue with their day.

"It looks as though we'll have another 'accident' to look into after all. When we get back, that is."

There was a mischievous twinkle in Marjorie's eye. Rachel groaned aloud.

"This can't be happening."

Chapter 5

Rachel and Marjorie enjoyed their visits to the main tourist attractions in Copenhagen, and Marjorie was particularly pleased that the Little Mermaid statue had been returned to her rightful place.

"She certainly is well named," remarked Rachel, surprised at how small the statue actually was. "I don't understand why, but I imagined she'd be bigger somehow."

"I was surprised too, the first time I saw her, but I expect that's why she's called the *Little* Mermaid," Marjorie teased.

After taking some photos, they wandered around the harbour for a while, watching the changing of the guard at the

Amalienborg Palace at midday before stopping for lunch.

"That was interesting, but I have to say the one at Buckingham Palace beats it by a country mile," commented Rachel.

"Ah yes, well that does take some beating. No-one does pomp and ceremony quite like the British – not that I'm biased. Here in Copenhagen, it is much more spectacular when the Danish queen is in residence, usually in the winter months."

The day glowed with brilliant sunlight and temperatures hovering around the twenty-two degree mark, making it pleasant but not too hot for Marjorie. Rachel recognised that her elderly friend looked tired after taking a walk around the Tivoli Gardens following lunch. Although still spritely for her eighty-six years and able to walk with the assistance of a stick for lengthy periods on the flat, she was slowing down.

"Would you like to return to the ship?"

"Not yet, dear. However, I am happy to rest a while. If we can find an English newspaper, you can park me at that hotel over there and then you can go exploring by yourself, if that's agreeable?"

They walked to the hotel near to the Tivoli Gardens and not too far from the river front. The concierge found a copy of the *Daily Telegraph* in English for Marjorie to read. After finding plush cushioned seats in the rather opulent lounge, Rachel ordered tea for the old lady.

"This reminds me of the ship's atrium," she remarked. "Are you certain you'll be alright?"

"Absolutely, I will catch up on the news from Blighty and enjoy a nice cup of tea. You go and enjoy yourself." Marjorie picked up the newspaper and soon became engrossed.

Rachel left the grand hotel and walked along the river front admiring the beautifully vibrant painted buildings that lined the area. She was considering returning to the hotel to join Marjorie when she heard English voices coming from a café to her right. There, seated at a table outside, she saw Brigitte and Gwen, Sarah's nurse colleagues, wearing mufti as they were obviously on shore leave for the day.

Gwen saw Rachel and stood up.

"Rachel, how nice to see you. Sarah told us you were on board with Lady Snellthorpe. Is she with you?" The Australian senior nurse gave Rachel a warm hug.

"We came out together, but I left her resting down the road at the Nimb Hotel while I did a bit more exploring."

Brigitte, the French nurse who Rachel had met on her first cruise, stood and gave her the traditional air kiss while touching each cheek, French style.

"Please join us, we were just about to order," Gwen invited.

Rachel sat down. "I will thank you."

Gwen handed her a menu. "What will you have? Our treat."

"Much appreciated. I guess as I'm in Denmark, I ought to have a Danish pastry."

"Ah, but which one?" Brigitte teased, going on to explain the many varieties of Danish pastry options while pointing out the more popular ones on the menu.

"Wow! I never knew that. I'm going to have the Snegl with cinnamon – that's the one I'm familiar with back home."

The waiter came to take their order.

"I'll have a croissant," Brigitte told him.

"And I'll have the Spandauer Danish, I love custard," Gwen explained. Rachel ordered her Snegl, and they all requested tea.

"How's your father?" Rachel asked Brigitte, aware he had been involved in a car accident the previous summer when the nurse had been called home at short notice.

"He is well now, thank you. Back to his normal bossy self so I'm glad to be back at sea."

"What about you, Rachel? How are you?" asked Gwen.

"I'm good, thanks. Started a new job in January – a new year, a fresh start. I'm working in north London, but living in a West End apartment thanks to Marjorie."

"That sounds expensive."

"It would be totally unaffordable, but Marjorie is glad to have someone living in it so she charges me a silly rent."

"I expect it's her way of paying you back for saving her life. How's the job in London, is it busy?"

"Incredibly, but I knew it would be when I took it. I'm working towards my sergeant's exams as well – glutton for punishment. The move to London means I'm closer to Carlos and following the near-miss and persistent threats from a man I helped put away for murder, it seemed like the right time to move." She had been a police constable for almost two years and still enjoyed her work, although it presented many challenges.

"I heard about that man. I do hope you don't have to use your sleuthing skills on this cruise." Brigitte laughed.

"We have been relatively quiet in terms of corpses," Gwen interjected light heartedly. "Since your last cruise, we haven't used the morgue next to the medical centre, but when Sarah said you were on board, Bernard warned us there was bound to be a body."

"Bernard has a wicked sense of humour." Rachel grimaced. "I guess you left the ship early this morning then?"

"You're not kidding! Yes, we like to take full advantage of shore leave when we get it," said Brigitte.

Gwen picked up on Rachel's serious expression and the guarded comment. "What do you mean by then? Has something happened?"

Rachel felt like a Grinch for upsetting the two nurses' day out, but explained what she and Marjorie had witnessed when standing at the dockside before leaving.

"Oh my goodness, Rachel! Did you find out what happened?" Brigitte exclaimed.

"No, we were ushered away pretty sharpish. A couple of officers dived into the water after the person – it appeared to be a man. In fact, I'm almost certain it was the lead singer of the Queen tribute band, Dom somebody or other, but that was only because of the white jumpsuit – it could have been anyone. I didn't notice which deck he fell from, but he wasn't flailing, which makes me wonder."

"I can't believe it," said Gwen, staring at Rachel closely as if to check whether she was winding them up.

Rachel shrugged her shoulders. "I seem to have that effect on the *Coral*."

"Do you think we should go back?" Brigitte asked Gwen.

"No, from what Rachel described, once he's dragged out of the water, he'll be transferred to hospital. If the worst has happened – well, we'll cross that bridge when we come to it."

Brigitte looked relieved. "In that case, I'm going to tuck in to my croissant," she said as the food arrived.

"What did you mean by that flailing remark, Rachel? Are you suggesting it wasn't an accident?" Gwen enquired.

"Not sure – it could have been. You know me, never satisfied unless there's a suspicious death to solve." Rachel could tell that Gwen wasn't convinced by the answer, but decided to stick with it as she didn't want to be responsible for ruining their day any more than she had already.

Rachel stayed with the two nurses for an hour, talking about other things, before deciding it was time to leave.

"I'd better go and find Marjorie in case she thinks I've got lost. It was lovely to meet you again – tell Sarah I'll meet her tonight."

"Will do. We're just going to visit an ice bar before returning to the ship."

"Oh, Sarah's hoping to take me to one of those when we get to Finland. Enjoy yourselves, I'm sure we'll catch up later."

Rachel left the two women and headed back to the Nimb Hotel. When she arrived, her friend was sitting comfortably, chatting to another elderly lady.

"There you are." Marjorie smiled. "I was wondering if I needed to send out a search party! Rachel, this is Gloria. Gloria's staying in Copenhagen for a week with her husband."

"How do you do?" Rachel greeted a short, casually dressed woman in her seventies. The woman had smiling blue eyes, dyed auburn hair and wore heavy makeup and lipstick.

"Hello there. Marjorie has been telling me all about you and your antics on board cruise ships." Gloria shook Rachel's hand, speaking with a pleasantly lilting

Welsh accent. Embarrassed, Rachel blushed – she didn't want to discuss murderous cruises. Marjorie understood and piped up.

"Well, it's time we returned to our trusty steed, Rachel. We don't want to miss the boat, now, do we?" She couldn't resist turning back to Gloria and whispering, "Especially when there's been another murder."

"Get away with you," rebuked Gloria, not sure whether to take Marjorie seriously.

Marjorie winked at Rachel and then pulled herself up from the seat, straightening herself to get her balance before taking Rachel's arm.

"Did you hear my bones creak then?" Not waiting for an answer, she turned to her new friend. "It was good to meet you, Gloria. Enjoy the rest of your stay. You chose the right hotel, I must say – the service has been excellent."

Gloria stood up and shook both women's hands. "It's been a pleasure, Marjorie, and don't forget, you'd be welcome in Carmarthen anytime."

"Thank you," answered Marjorie. Turning to Rachel as they left the hotel, she asked, "Did you have a nice time?"

"I did, I took a lovely walk along the river and bumped into Gwen and Brigitte. Do you remember them? They asked after you."

"I do remember them, very well. Brigitte is the French nurse who looked after me when I was in the infirmary and Gwen is the Sister. There's nothing wrong with these grey cells yet. Have they ascertained what happened to the person who fell overboard?"

"No, they didn't even know about it – they left early to ensure they got a full day out, but Gwen says that he would most likely be admitted to hospital in Copenhagen if he survived the fall, so nothing for them to worry about. If it was a fall."

"Oh no, Rachel, surely not? I was only joking when I said we would need to investigate, but I can see you've got that look in your eye." Marjorie smiled up at Rachel. "You don't think he fell at all, do you?"

Rachel was thoughtful. She had been pondering the man overboard scene they had witnessed and rewinding it over and over in her mind.

"I can't be certain, but no, he plummeted too quietly and too quickly. In fact, if it hadn't been for that woman gasping and our line of sight, no-one would have even noticed."

Marjorie sensed Rachel's need to mull things over in her mind and squeezed her arm before sighing.

"Let's get back, then, shall we?"

It was only after speaking about the falling man to Gwen and Brigitte, and now Marjorie that Rachel had come to the conclusion that he was probably unconscious when he went overboard. She would want to discuss it with the chief of security, Jack Waverley, whom she had met on the two previous cruises that turned out to be deadly. Waverley and Rachel had developed a mutual respect, although he wasn't always happy with her involvement in his investigations – the main reason being her passenger status. He'd offered her a job on his security team on both occasions, but she had declined. There were times when she would love to be working as a security officer on a cruise ship with the travel opportunities that it offered, but she had initially felt the need to consolidate her police training with practical work, and more recently she hated the thought of being away from Carlos for the amount of time that would be required if she took up this line of work. Carlos worked as a private investigator, and although this meant he travelled away at times, most cruise ship contracts were six to nine months.

On arriving back at the *Coral Queen*, Rachel and Marjorie discovered all was normal.

"You wouldn't imagine anything had happened this morning," remarked Marjorie.

Rachel could see exactly what she meant. Passengers were returning to the ship, and the crew welcomed them back with iced flannels and refreshments, just as they always did before the passengers climbed the steps to pass through security on rejoining the ship. It was surreal in many ways, considering what they had witnessed just six hours ago.

"If we hadn't seen it with our own eyes, we just wouldn't know," said Rachel, taking in a deep breath. Instead of heading for the gangway and steps, they walked to the front of the ship where they had seen the man fall. All was calm in the dark black water; Rachel spotted fish swimming near to the surface, but other than that, it was pretty murky.

Probably polluted from all the ships sailing in and out of the harbour.

Rachel looked upwards, re-enacting the scene in her mind's eye, but try as she might, she couldn't determine which deck he'd fallen from.

"Definitely higher than deck twelve," she said out loud. "The top of that crane was about level with him when I spotted him falling. He was also higher than that suspended platform there where the crewman is painting. Although he's moved around from where he was this morning, he's at the same level."

"Yes, I noticed him too," said Marjorie. "I remember thinking to myself that the crew always seems to be painting something or other outside when the ship is docked. I imagine cruise ships are painted more than any other vessel. Do you suppose it's necessary or to give them something to do?"

"You're right, now you mention it, there is always painting going on. I expect it's to stop corrosion from the salt water and other pollutants." Rachel's mind was elsewhere. She was only half concentrating on the topic of ship maintenance procedures as she was still picturing the falling body from this morning. "I wonder if that crewman noticed anything. He's quite high up so he might have."

"I doubt it, my dear, listen to all that racket going on from those cranes working over there, and the machinery was hard at it this morning. They began at eight o'clock when I sat on my balcony, and we're at the back of the ship where there isn't as much activity as there is here."

Rachel was disappointed, but agreed with Marjorie's logic. With all the banging and clanging around the dockside from cargo vessels being loaded and unloaded, it would be unlikely the crewman had noticed anything. Nevertheless, she zoomed in on him with the camera on her mobile phone and took a picture, just in case she needed to track him down later.

She showed the image of two men dressed in white overalls to Marjorie. "Technology these days is marvellous," declared the elderly lady. "I can't believe your phone can capture those dots of men with such clarity. They look like they are from the Philippines to me. Many cruise ship workers come from there."

"Agreed. I'll ask Chief Waverley if I need to, but I suspect you're right about them not hearing anything – when I zoom in, I can see they appear to be shouting to each other over the noise." She snapped a couple more photos of the front of the ship, and then noticed people staring down at her from their balconies. "Come on, Marjorie. Time to get back on board."

Passing through security, Rachel spotted Waverley speaking to two other guards. He saw her coming through.

"Miss Prince – I gathered you were on board. Lady Snellthorpe – what a pleasure it is to see you again."

Marjorie answered first. "Thank you, I feel much more secure now I've seen you." Rachel detected a hint of sarcasm in her voice.

Waverley coughed, as he seemed to do when nervous or distracted. "We do our best," he mumbled.

"What happened to that person we saw fall from the ship this morning?" Marjorie had him under the cosh and wasn't going to let up any time soon.

He coughed again, and this time his neck reddened. He looked towards Rachel for help. "Erm. I didn't realise you had witnessed that event. Perhaps we can talk about this later?"

Rachel noticed a large group of passengers were passing through security behind them. "Yes, we can do that. Come on, Marjorie, we'd better go and get ready for dinner."

Marjorie was chuckling like a naughty schoolgirl as they got into the lift. Rachel had to smile.

Once they'd got off on deck fifteen, Rachel spoke. "I suspected you had a darker side, Lady Marjorie Snellthorpe – the poor man didn't know where to put himself."

Marjorie was still chuckling. "Serves him right for bungling things up previously." She was referring to the cruise when they had originally met and Waverley had had Marjorie followed for a while.

"To be fair, it wasn't just Chief Waverley that messed up. Carlos wasn't great either, though I hate to admit it."

"Ah, but I can forgive him because he's a handsome young man, and he's made up for it since."

"I can see you're going to be incorrigible over the next few days," said Rachel, laughing.

Rachel walked Marjorie to her room and then crossed the rear corridor to her own suite. The luxury suites were magnificent. She appreciated the exquisite decor and the facilities were second to none. The suite had as much space as her apartment at home. The large sitting room overlooked one part of the balcony and the bedroom led out on to the other half, providing ample space for at least six people to sit outside in comfort. The suites were served by the butler, Mario, and he looked after them well.

She helped herself to a glass of mineral water from the well-stocked fridge and opened the doors to the balcony as her mobile phone rang with Carlos's designated ringtone.

"Carlos, hi." Her voice took on an endearing high-pitched note.

"Hello, darling. I knew you were on land today and wanted to hear the sound of your voice."

"It's wonderful you phoned. How are things?"

"Not too bad, I'm in Birmingham looking for a missing dog – stolen from a house in your neck of the woods, Knightsbridge. I've tracked the person who has it and I'm closing in. Lady's with me."

Lady was Carlos's two-year-old Springer Spaniel, a recent acquisition from a friend who'd emigrated, and she now accompanied him on his investigative tours. The two of them had become inseparable, and Rachel had grown almost as fond of the dog as Carlos was.

"Oh, I do hope you find the dog you're looking for. Why was it stolen?"

"Stolen to order. It's a golden retriever puppy from a champion breeder. The family is distraught, as you can imagine – the dog had become the children's pet, but I'm pretty confident I can get it back by tomorrow. Lady and I are going to pay a visit to the thief in an hour."

"Be careful, Carlos."

"Don't worry, darling. I've got a detective pal of mine meeting me at the house, ready to arrest the thief if he doesn't tell us where the dog is. Lady will sniff it out if it's in the house, but he'll have passed it on for sure. Anyway, that's enough about me. How's your cruise? Please tell me there are no dead bodies."

Rachel swallowed hard as she answered. She'd promised him after the last cruise that she would tell him everything in future because he hadn't known she'd been in danger. He'd been desperately unhappy she hadn't told him what was happening at the time.

"I don't think so—"

"*Mamma Mia!* Rachel – it can't happen three cruises in a row."

"As I say, I'm not certain, but Marjorie and I witnessed someone fall over the side when we were leaving the ship this morning, before we were ushered away. I don't know exactly what happened to the person. It was probably an accident anyway." *Surely one white lie couldn't hurt?*

It was quiet at the other end of the phone for a moment, but Carlos sounded more chipper when he spoke again.

"Well at least that won't involve you, whatever happened. Probably someone showing off to their mates."

"Could have been, and you're right, it doesn't involve me."

The line started to fade.

"The connection's bad now, Rachel, and I have to get ready to leave. Take care and enjoy yourself. Stay out of trouble."

"You too, and give Lady a treat from me. Bye."

Carlos hung up and Rachel kissed the phone automatically. Then her thoughts turned back to the body over the side situation.

Chapter 6

Following an exceptional five-course dining extravaganza in the *Coral* restaurant, Rachel and Marjorie met up with Sarah.

"Have you eaten?" Rachel asked.

"Yes, I grabbed a quick bite from the buffet. I suppose the pair of you dined well?"

"I must say, the lobster tasted exquisite," said Marjorie.

Sarah raised her eyebrows.

"Personally, I'm stuffed," said Rachel. "The chefs should be arrested for cooking up such irresistible cuisine."

"Since I became a cruise ship nurse, my culinary tastes have been extended beyond belief. Not always positively, but mostly so."

"Oh, do tell, what don't you like?" asked Marjorie.

"Well, durian certainly isn't my favourite."

Rachel looked confused.

"Oh, the fruit, you mean. It's popular in south-east Asia, isn't it?" said Marjorie.

"Yes, and you smell it before you see it. I could never enjoy it because it smells so foul. I did try a very small piece in Malaysia. The catering department doesn't bring it on board for obvious reasons."

The three women discussed food and drink as they made their way to an early evening show. The theatre at the front of the ship boasted luxurious tiered seating spanning two decks. They commandeered three seats at the rear so that Marjorie didn't need to negotiate too many steps. No-one mentioned the man overboard situation and Rachel could feel the elephant moving into the room.

"I met Gwen and Brigitte along the Nyhavn today," she prompted.

"Did you?" said Sarah. "I haven't seen them since they got back on board. I was on call, and they were in surgery when I handed the on-call bag over to Bernard for the night. That's why I only managed a rushed dinner."

That explains it. She obviously isn't aware we saw the man go overboard.

"I expect you were busy after the accident this morning," whispered Marjorie.

The troubled look on Sarah's face confirmed what Rachel had supposed. "How do you know about that?" she asked quietly.

"We witnessed it, didn't we, Rachel?"

"Yes, it happened just as we were leaving the ship." Rachel shot an apologetic glance at her friend.

"I'd hoped to keep you out of this one," groaned Sarah. "But I suppose you might have found out anyway."

Their conversation was interrupted as the cruise director Gordon appeared on stage and introduced the evening's main act, a singer who'd been on *America's got Talent*.

"Shall we talk about it afterwards?" whispered Rachel.

Sarah nodded.

Although the singing sounded respectable enough, Rachel found her mind drifting back to the morning and replaying various scenarios over in her head – drunken fall, bravado as Carlos thought, or push? It had looked like the Freddie Mercury lookalike, but it could have been another member of the band, or anyone else wearing a white jumpsuit for that matter.

Sarah ordered drinks, and when they arrived Rachel absentmindedly took hers from the waiter, before telling herself to switch off and enjoy the show – she would find out soon enough what had occurred.

The rest of the performance passed by in a blur until raucous applause brought Rachel back to the present. Sarah nudged her to move as they were blocking the aisle and people wanted to leave the auditorium. Marjorie looked happy.

"What a delightful evening. I've had a lovely day, but if you two young things don't mind, it's time for this old lady to retire. I expect you have things to talk about." Marjorie winked.

Rachel kissed Marjorie on the cheek after she and Sarah had escorted her to the lifts in the midships area.

"Goodnight, Marjorie. See you in the morning."

"Goodnight, Rachel. Goodnight, Sarah."

Sarah kissed her too, and then the two young women made their way to the Jazz Bar, one of the many bars aboard the *Coral Queen*, which also happened to be one of their favourite haunts, although the lively bar didn't provide a good opportunity to talk thanks to the volume of the music. Rachel suspected Sarah's desperation to keep her out of another investigation confirmed that the man overboard scenario was suspicious. If not, she would have said something.

They ordered drinks, Sarah asking for cola while Rachel had a martini and lemonade. Then Rachel gave Sarah a look.

"You're going to need to talk about it sometime."

Sarah led her towards the edge of the room where they claimed a booth from people just leaving.

"It was the lead singer from the tribute band."

"Was? That means he's dead then."

"Yes. They pulled him out barely alive, and after resuscitation and first aid, they took him to hospital, but he died shortly afterwards."

"Were you involved?" Rachel sympathised with Sarah, who looked shattered.

"We all were. We managed to get him round before the ambulance came, but he died of a brain haemorrhage."

"Is that unusual?"

"It could have been caused by his head hitting the water after falling from a great height, but witnesses believe he was unconscious when he fell."

"Yes, I thought the same. He just dropped like an inanimate object."

"It gets worse." Sarah looked around for a brief moment, checking no-one was listening. "He's the new cruise director's brother – that's how the band got the job, apparently. The entertainment officer, Rosa Doherty, is none too pleased as she didn't like Dom, or any of them, from the off. She wanted to sack them – she's had numerous complaints about them from female crew members, and some from passengers. What's more, Alex spent the night patching a few of them up following a brawl in their manager's room."

Alessandro Romano, better known as Alex, was the ship's junior doctor. Rachel had met him previously and liked him.

"I didn't realise they were brothers. When you told me their names before, it didn't register they had the same surname.

So there could be a motive among his band mates, if this is murder?"

"That's the only reason they haven't been sacked and escorted off the ship. Rosa wanted to give them the push this morning, but in view of events, Waverley says they must stay."

"Any idea what Waverley thinks?"

"No, he hasn't been near us today. From a distance, he looked stressed to say the least. He's been busy interviewing distressed passengers who witnessed the fall. The security team has also been stretched due to a rowdy stag party who have been causing trouble with a group of cheerleaders. Jason says the chief's at the end of his tether."

"Oh dear – and then Marjorie made things worse with a pointed jibe." Sarah looked confused. "She goaded him a bit over the incident, still miffed with him for having her followed on her last cruise."

"Poor Waverley." Sarah laughed. "He doesn't ever get an easy time of it, but it always seems much worse when you're on board. If you don't take him up on his job offer soon, he might ban you from travelling on the *Coral Queen* altogether."

Rachel feigned offence. "I can't be responsible for every crime committed on board this ship! Anyway, this one's nothing to do with me."

"You don't fool me, Rachel Prince – you can't resist a challenge. You will start sleuthing soon, if you haven't already." Sarah smiled grimly. "Just don't put yourself in danger, and remember you've got Marjorie to take care of. She's a frail old lady and the excitement won't be good for her."

"Bah! There's nothing frail about Marjorie – she's as tough as old boots, in the nicest possible sense. Anyway, she's already keen to get going on this – she's arranged for us to hold a war council in the morning so we can come up with an investigative action plan."

Sarah looked exasperated. "I don't know who's worse – you or her."

Rachel gave a mischievous smile and then said more seriously, "I will take care of her. I'm not looking for trouble, but we might do a bit of snooping. I feel sorry for Waverley and he might need my help."

"I don't think he'll see it that way, but I'll find out what I can from Jason, as long as you promise you won't do anything dangerous."

"Guides' honour," answered Rachel.

"Hey, you two." Bernard's cheerful voice cut them off.

"Bernard, great to meet you again." Bernard and Rachel hugged while Sarah moved along the bench seat to let him in.

"How can someone get more beautiful each time we meet?" Bernard said.

Sarah glared at him, knowing how fed up Rachel got with men constantly drawing attention to her looks, but Bernard remained oblivious. He was one of the few men who didn't attract a cutting remark in return.

"I thought you were on call tonight," Sarah said.

"I thought so too, but Gwen offered to do it because of the day we've had."

"That's nice of her," replied Sarah.

"Did you hear about our day, Rachel?" He leaned in. "I guess you heard the one about the singer in the drink?"

"Bernard, that's horrible!" Sarah admonished.

"Sarah's just been telling me about it – I understand the grapevine suggests it might not have been an accident."

Bernard giggled. "Well, it wouldn't be with you on board, would it?"

"I don't understand why everyone surmises it's anything to do with me!" She laughed. "It's your screening that's gone to pot – obviously you just let anyone on board cruise ships nowadays."

Following a period of banter, Bernard turned more serious. "The brawl last night sounds worse than we first believed."

"What do you mean?" asked Sarah.

"We imagined it to be a drunken argument that got out of hand, but according to my source, it was nastier than that. It turns out Dominic Venables had quite a few enemies, not least those in his own band. There were women involved too, with one of them swearing she'd kill him if he didn't get his act together."

"What women? They must have been crew if they were below the waterline."

"My source didn't see them, just heard the racket and told them to shut up or she'd report them. Poor girl works in housekeeping and was exhausted, says they were really loud."

Rachel listened intently. "That's a shame she doesn't know who they are. Do you know if any of the men were up top at the time of the incident this morning?"

"Graham says they all deny being up there and none of them have decent alibis."

"Oh, so Graham's getting the sleuthing bug now, is he?" said Sarah, clearly ruffled. "Really, I can't wait to hear what Waverley makes of that. What's the matter with you lot?"

Rachel laughed at her friend's angst and understood it to be concern over her getting involved following a few near misses in the past. A pacifist through and through, Sarah hated violence, although she'd witnessed her fair share as a nurse working in casualty on land and on a cruise ship. Nevertheless, she just wanted people to get along with each other and had always wanted to repair rather than destroy, a trait responsible for her becoming a nurse.

Bernard answered, "No worries there. Graham got the message last time, but he took Waverley for dinner tonight to try to help him relax after the day he's had. He also had to report all injuries sustained by passengers and crew over the past twenty-four hours in case they're related."

Rachel put her hand on her friend's arm. "Don't worry, Sarah, it'll be okay – sounds like some internal squabbling that's got out of hand, so at least there's not a killer running loose intent on inflicting random acts of violence or looking for more victims."

Sarah nodded. "I'm sorry, but I will never be able to understand the mindset of a killer – death is so final—" Her voice

trailed off and alarm bells sounded for
Rachel – there was something else on
Sarah's mind she hadn't shared.

Now I'm worried.

They finished their drinks, said
goodnight to Bernard, and took a stroll
around the upper decks. Sarah explained
that security had confirmed the man fell
from the front of deck sixteen, so Rachel
suggested they visit the would-be crime
scene. No-one on the bridge had seen the
incident because they were relaxing while
the ship remained docked.

The deck appeared relatively quiet
when they arrived as most of the action
was occurring in the bars and lounges,
although they encountered a few couples
taking moonlight strolls. The sounds of
distant music emanated from the ship's
decks, but the most striking sound, the
one that Rachel loved, came from waves
sloshing against the side of the ship. As

they were at sea again, the enormous vessel was tunnelling her way through the waves, her path resulting in the crashing noise as the waves objected. It was the most beautiful thing about night-time cruising and more pronounced at the bow of the ship.

"Oh, Sarah, look at the stars!" For a brief moment, they lost themselves in the beauty of the world around them. The water was pitch black and eerie beneath them, while the night sky above produced a glorious darkness, broken by the light from innumerable twinkling stars.

"I love nights like this," said Sarah. "They make me happy to be a cruise ship nurse. Sometimes I get to be wonderfully alone, in spite of the five thousand odd people on board. It makes me glad to be alive."

Another reference to life and death. Rachel felt anxiety about her friend. What could be making Sarah so morose? She needed to find out and help her.

"I know what you mean – it is rather special."

Their reverie was interrupted by the sounds of laughter as a group emerged from a door behind them and headed off towards the stern.

"I'd better show you where it all happened before you burst."

"Okay, thanks. Where do they say he fell from?"

"Port side, bow."

Sarah led the way and Rachel followed. Port referred to the left-hand side of the ship when facing forward as frequently it was this side of the ship that docked against a port's side. On this occasion, the ship had been docked starboard side in Copenhagen. No sign of what may have occurred just this morning jumped out at them. Rachel noticed a buoy tied to the rail and wondered if it had been thrown in the water after the man. A thought she dismissed as unlikely if they were looking at murder. *Besides,* she told herself, *it came from a lower deck.*

Sarah answered her unasked question.

"A buoy was thrown from deck twelve, not from here."

"It's looking more and more like murder," Rachel said thoughtfully.

They snooped around, but it was obvious they were not going to find any evidence. Waverley would have already done a sweep of the whole area and interviewed anyone in the vicinity at the time of the incident. No scuff marks were visible on the railings where Venables was reported to have gone over.

Rachel looked downwards and gasped, contemplating plunging into the depths from this height. She imagined that even if conscious, one might not survive such a fall. Looking at her watch, she realised it was after midnight and suddenly felt tired, but instead of saying goodnight, she turned to her friend and gently asked a question.

"Sarah, is something else bothering you?"

Sarah bit her lip, a sign of stress that Rachel recognised from their student days. She looked out to sea and Rachel watched the tears trickling down her cheeks.

"You'll think I'm silly," she said quietly.

Rachel joined her by the rail and put her arm around her. "Whatever is troubling you is not silly."

"Mum Skyped this morning to ask if they could have Pickles put down." Tears were now flowing freely down her face, causing tracks to form through her light foundation. "He's riddled with cancer and the vet said there's no more she can do. It seems trivial in the light of the death of a man on board, but I can't help it."

Rachel embraced her sobbing friend, who cried on her shoulder.

"I'm so sorry, Sarah, and it's not trivial. Pickles has been part of your family for eighteen years." Rachel remembered the little kitten being bought for her friend's eighth birthday and how he'd looked so much like a jar of pickle that Sarah had hugged him and named him Pickles. The Bradshaw family often joked about how he was more like a dog than a cat – he lacked the independence and aloofness of some cats and followed Sarah around whenever she visited home.

"They took him this afternoon," Sarah sobbed into Rachel's shoulder. There was little Rachel could say to console her friend. To Sarah, it was like losing a member of the family.

Sarah eventually stopped crying and wiped her eyes. "At least I got to see him one more time via Skype. Mum had him sitting on her knee. She'll be even more upset than I am, having looked after him since I've lived away for so long. Now I feel guilty for taking this job and not being there."

A chill developed in the night air as if it understood the significance of the moment. Sarah shivered.

"Come on, let's get you inside. I am truly sorry, Sarah. I'll pray for you and your family tonight."

"I'd appreciate that, Rachel. I'm going to call it a night. I'll catch you tomorrow."

Rachel watched her get into the lift at the front of the ship before walking towards the stern to make her way back to her own room.

Poor Sarah, what a day!

Chapter 7

Mario brought tea and coffee through to Marjorie's room where Rachel had joined the old lady on her extensive balcony. An early morning run around deck sixteen and forty-five minutes in the gym had left Rachel feeling invigorated. They had a sea day ahead so they could take their leisure.

Marjorie looked tired and a little pale. Rachel hoped she wasn't going down with anything.

"Are you alright?" she asked.

"Yes, dear, although I can't say I slept well last night. One of those disturbed nights, I'm afraid."

"I had a message from Chief Waverley. He would like to speak to us this morning. Would you like me to ask him to come up here or shall we venture down to his office?"

"Oh, make him come up here, it will give us home advantage."

"Okay, up here it is. Are you coming down for breakfast?"

"No, I think I'll eat out here on the balcony. You go off to the buffet, I know you prefer to eat there during the day."

"I'll just call Waverley before I leave."

Waverley agreed to meet them in Marjorie's room at 10am, giving Rachel time to shower, change out of her running gear and eat before he arrived. She made her way up to the buffet for breakfast before returning to Marjorie's room to wait with the old lady, who looked more like her normal self again, for the security chief.

At precisely 10am the expected knock came and Rachel opened the door. On close inspection, Waverley looked almost the same as he had done on her two previous cruises, tall with short greying hair, now thinning on top. A burly ex-navy officer, he had been chief of security for over a decade. But Rachel noticed some weight gain around the middle. His usually ruddy face appeared pallid beneath the tan, as if he hadn't been sleeping well, and there were dark lines under his penetrating deep-brown eyes.

"Chief Waverley, good to see you, please come in."

He followed Rachel outside to the balcony where Marjorie was enjoying the morning sun. Marjorie stood and invited him to sit down before doing so herself.

"Thank you for seeing me, ladies."

A second knock followed and Mario entered with a flask of fresh coffee and biscuits.

"I took the liberty of ordering coffee," explained Marjorie.

"Thank you." Waverley blushed and coughed, and Rachel wondered if he might still be smarting from Marjorie's barbs the day before.

"I'll try not to intrude on your day and won't keep you too long. I'm interviewing all passengers and crew who witnessed the tragic event that took place yesterday morning, and as Lady Snellthorpe indicated that you had both seen the man falling, I wanted to speak with you."

"What would you like to know?" asked Marjorie, clearly enjoying the chief's discomfort.

"Could you both describe what you remember about the incident?"

Rachel explained what they had witnessed and how the man appeared to plummet into the sea like a brick from on high. "I've gone over it a lot and it looked to me like he was unconscious before he went in. Of course, if it was suicide he may have chosen to dive in like that, but it certainly didn't strike me as a fall."

"Do you feel the same, Lady Snellthorpe?"

"Yes, I'm afraid I do. The poor man didn't cry out or anything, and I'm sure he would have done so if he'd fallen, unless of course he was so inebriated he didn't realise what was happening. Judging by the man's previous behaviour, intoxication wouldn't be completely out of the question."

"I understand you met him in the Rat Pack bar the night before he died."

"I would say encountered, rather than met. We certainly weren't introduced. The man was drunk and annoying Rachel, but she dealt with him quite admirably." Marjorie snickered.

"So I understand." Waverley looked at Rachel admiringly. "Did he have any bruises to his face when you, erm, encountered him?"

"No," answered Rachel, "although he had a lot of makeup on which might have masked bruising. He didn't appear to have any later either when Sarah and I watched the band play in the Culture Lounge. I did spot him arguing with the lead guitarist, though."

Waverley looked up from writing notes. "Do you have any idea what the argument was about? A few passengers mentioned seeing the two men argue but couldn't recall any details."

"Venables shouted at the lead guitarist – I think it was him – accusing him of trying to take over as lead singer, followed by a rant about the rest of the band back-biting about him. I put it down to rivalry and paranoia. I only overheard them because Sarah had nipped into the ladies and I was waiting nearby. He then barged right through me – I've still got the bruise on my shoulder to show for it."

"I didn't know that," said Marjorie, shocked. "Horrible man. He was a rather unpleasant fellow, Chief Waverley, but obviously I'm sorry that he is dead."

"You heard he's dead, then? Sarah, I suppose." He didn't wait for a reply. "Yes, he died in the ambulance before arriving at the hospital, a brain haemorrhage. There will be a post-mortem today, but initial examination does point to him being unconscious or semi-conscious when he entered the water."

"Do you know who wanted him dead?" asked Rachel.

"There's a queue of people. From what I can gather, the band often argued, but they've been together for eighteen years and the arguing happens to be part of who they are – totally harmless, according to

Jimmy, their agent and manager who's also on board. Mr Venables managed to upset a few of the passengers, mainly due to drink and a bit of unwelcome fraternising, although I can't imagine a passenger killing him for that. To be honest, the entertainment manager was going to sack them yesterday morning, but then all this happened so she's had to keep them on at my insistence.

"My theory is a fight turned nasty, resulting in him ending up in the water. I haven't ruled out a drink-induced accident or suicide either. No-one in the band seems to have a clear alibi for the time of the incident so that hasn't helped narrow it down any." Waverley paused before giving Rachel a firm stare. "I would thank you to keep out of this one, Miss Prince. Leave it to the security team. We know what we're doing."

Marjorie made a choking sound and they both looked at her. Waverley looked concerned, but Rachel recognised from the twinkle in her eye that she was stifling a giggle.

"No problem, Chief, Rachel and I will forget all about the incident," she said sincerely.

"Thank you. I will not take up any more of your time. Have a pleasant day, ladies."

Rachel escorted him to the door. He looked at her again. "I mean it, Rachel. Stay out of it." He marched off down the corridor.

Rachel re-joined Marjorie who was now guffawing, which made Rachel laugh too. Once they'd stopped laughing like a pair of teenagers, Marjorie sat up straight.

"We need an action plan – first, let's write down our list of suspects."

"Maybe we should take his advice and stay out of it."

"We should," said Marjorie. "But we're not going to, are we, dear?" A disappointed frown appeared on her face.

"Well, I guess he might need our help, even if he doesn't realise it," sighed Rachel, cursing herself for ever having seen the man fall overboard in the first place. Carlos was not going to like it, but she couldn't resist doing a little bit of undercover investigating. She nodded to Marjorie, having made up her mind.

"Right then, who's our chief suspect?" asked Marjorie, taking out a pen and notebook from her handbag.

"The lead guitarist would have to be in the frame – he's the one who argued with Venables in the club, and it seems like a deep-seated rivalry or jealousy existed between them. Jealousy is always a good motive."

Marjorie wrote in her book, and then said, "Jealousy and money. There's also the agent."

"Or any of the other band members. We don't have enough information about them. We need to track them down and poke around a bit. I'll ask Sarah later for some more detail about the room brawl and who was involved in that. Bernard said a woman threatened him, but no-one knows who she is." Rachel paused. "It's interesting they still plan to perform, isn't it?"

"Typical of these entertainment types," said Marjorie. "*The Show Must Go On* – wasn't that a Queen song? Seems rather apt. It's in their genetics, unless, of course, they really don't care about the man's death. He certainly seems to have had more enemies than friends, and from what we experienced of him, it's not hard to imagine why."

"That might be right, but they're a heartless group of people if it's true. We'll need to find out when they next perform and where."

Marjorie picked up the day's copy of *Coral News* and scrolled through. "They're doing two evening shows in the Culture Lounge, one at eight and one at eleven. They're also doing a live show on the lido deck at two o'clock. Oh please, let's go to that one – the noise will be more tolerable in the open air."

Rachel nodded agreement. "That gives us a few hours this morning. What would you like to do?"

"There's a quiz at eleven in the Sky View Lounge, would you be happy to accompany an old lady to that?"

"Absolutely, let's go."

They made their way up to deck sixteen and entered the Sky View, situated at the bow of the ship. It spread across the whole deck with spectacular views of the sea from full height windows that enfolded the room in a semicircle. A glitzy circular bar dominated the centre of the room. Marble-topped tables were scattered throughout and avid quizzers arriving early settled in their teams. Gentle music played in the background.

Marjorie nudged Rachel. "Over there," she whispered.

Rachel looked over to the opposite side of the room from where they had entered and followed Marjorie's gaze to where the members of the tribute band and their entourage were having an animated conversation. The two women made their way across the room to where the band was seated on a horseshoe sofa with two round tables in front of them, laden with drinks. The rest of the party sat on stools around the tables. Marjorie walked towards a table in close proximity, facing the horseshoe.

"There's room for two here, Rachel."

One of the men in the band looked up, but then ignored them as they sat on cushioned armchairs. A waiter came along and took their drinks order, Rachel asking for lemonade and Marjorie ordering tea.

The three band members sat next to each other. Rachel recognised them from the show two nights ago. She pointed them out to Marjorie.

"The one on the left is the bass guitarist, alias John Deacon."

"He's rather dashing, isn't he?"

Rachel had to agree, the tall muscular man, who she guessed at being in his late thirties, was the best looking of the bunch. With long brown thinly permed afro hair, he wore a denim shirt with cropped jeans showing off his muscular calves. He stood out among the contingent for his good looks, and also appeared quieter than the rest.

"The one in the middle, doing most of the talking, is the lead guitarist, alias Brian May."

From what she could gather from the conversation, he was making frequent scathing and sarcastic remarks to the others. He was around six foot with long, wavy dark brown hair and bronzed skin, wearing jeans and ripped t-shirt exposing heavily tattooed arms and overly hairy chest.

"That tan looks like it came out of a bottle, and do you think he takes hormones? That hair!" whispered Marjorie. Rachel laughed, but had to agree. "He seems as nasty as the other one, suits the Neanderthal appearance," Marjorie continued as the man yelled at one of the waiters. "Uncouth, too – I haven't heard language like that since boarding school."

"The guy on the right is the drummer, alias Roger Taylor, and I assume the man in the suit is the agent." The drummer looked to be the oldest in the group, early fifties, Rachel thought. He had long crinkly greying hair, a grey moustache and wore horn-rimmed glasses. His shirt was open to the waist, displaying a smooth and shiny six pack.

"My goodness, whatever cream he's using on that chest, I want some." Marjorie was clearly enjoying playing amateur detective and made notes in her notebook. "He's the only one who doesn't take the lookalike aspect too seriously, methinks. My observations lead me to suspect it's either the uncouth one or the agent."

"If only it was as simple as identifying a murderer by their looks," said Rachel.

"The agent looks shifty, though. What's he trying to do with that gum?"

They looked at a pot-bellied man in his mid-forties with ash brown crew-cut hair who, despite wearing a smart white suit, still looked bedraggled. He wore a gold stud earring, a bright yellow shirt, and was chewing gum aggressively, doing battle with the substance in his mouth.

An announcement came over the microphone to invite quizzers to collect quiz answer sheets from the assistant cruise director. The cruise director sat at the bar, so Rachel asked Marjorie to keep listening in to the band's conversation while she went over. After picking up one of the sheets and a pen from another crew member, Rachel made her way to the bar and ordered a drink she didn't need.

Gordon was slumped up against the bar on a bar stool, wearing a navy blue suit and a badge with his name and title displayed. His mouth smiled at her from beneath pained brown eyes, causing her heart to go out to him. The poor man had just lost his brother and had to continue performing his duty as director of entertainment for thousands of passengers seeking a good time. It was a big ask.

"Hello," she said. "We haven't met, but I'm Rachel, a friend of Sarah Bradshaw, one of the nurses."

"Gordon, I'm the new cruise director. Are you enjoying your cruise, Rachel?"

"So far, yes. Thank you." She thought about whether to broach the subject of his brother, but decided against it. She didn't want to upset him in a public lounge.

The assistant cruise director tapped him on the shoulder. "Sorry, Gordon, I need to get to the ballroom. Here's the list."

"Excuse me, Miss – hopefully we'll meet again."

Gordon took a deep breath and stoically made his way over to the microphone. Rachel went back to re-join Marjorie as the quiz was about to start.

They spent the next hour writing down answers to quiz questions, doing reasonably well, but not nearly as well as some of the teams who appeared to take the whole thing too seriously. The tribute band weren't taking part in the quiz, and at times became too raucous, causing passengers around them to hush them and attracting a scowl from Gordon. After being told off by an elderly gentleman nearby for the third time, the band and their hangers-on sauntered out of the lounge, still chatting loudly.

The winning team received prizes of a bottle of wine and a box of chocolates. Gordon acquitted himself well considering the pressure he must have been under, and came across as a natural entertainer. Following the conclusion of the quiz, pens were returned, and Gordon hastily marched out of the lounge.

"Did you glean anything from the brother?" Marjorie asked.

"No, I couldn't bring myself to broach the subject – not the right time or place. I did introduce myself as Sarah's friend. He looked pained, but something in his look bothered me. It was more angry pain than sad pain."

"There are many stages of grief and anger is one of them." Marjorie's voice trailed off and Rachel suspected she was referring to her own grief over the loss of her husband.

"You're right," Rachel said. "Did you pick up anything from the band's conversation?"

"Not really – they spoke a lot of drivel about girls, nightclubs and songs. Not a mention of the dead man. They don't appear or sound in the least bit sad. I don't suppose we'll be seeing any stages of grief among that lot. The only one that did seem out of sorts was the bass guitarist, who strikes me as a gentle giant – quietly spoken and not given to the verbal diarrhoea of the others."

"Perhaps he's the one we need to try to speak to," said Rachel.

"Agreed; he might even have a touch of sensitivity. Oh, the other thing I picked up is a new band member will be joining them tomorrow in Estonia. He's apparently not really new, more an old band member that had a fall out with someone – we can probably guess who – and is happy to help them out now."

"Good work, Marjorie. You have an eye for this sleuthing malarkey – now what say we go and get some lunch?"

"Yes please," Marjorie replied happily, seeming pleased with the compliment.

Chapter 8

The well-stocked buffet sported a dedicated theme each day as well as offering foods from around the world. Rachel and Marjorie filled their trays and ate outside. Afterwards, they made their way to the lido deck. They chose a table revealing a good view of the stage, but away from the giant overhead loudspeakers.

The deck was buzzing with activity along with happy splashes from the sparkling blue pools where children and adults vied for space. The Jacuzzi was being commandeered by a group of middle-aged women whose eyes fired daggers at a young couple daring to attempt entry. Meaty aromas from the grill bar on the next deck up wafted down to where they sat.

Rachel surveyed the rest of her surroundings. White peppery clouds formed overhead, but the sun was winning the battle thus far and the temperature had risen to a pleasant twenty-three degrees. The shouts and laughter from the pools and sun loungers surrounding them drowned out any sound of the sea waves that rocked the ship gently to and fro.

Shortly after they arrived, a game of water volleyball started up in the main pool. The teams consisted of officers versus crew with Gordon, the cruise director, providing a running commentary via a microphone. Among the officers playing was Alex, the junior doctor, and Rachel recognised Jason, Sarah's beau. The deputy captain and chief engineer also played in the officers' team. Gordon introduced the crew team that included two male dancers from the on-board dance troupe, an electrician and a maintenance engineer. Waverley was nowhere to be seen, but he didn't strike her as the pool game type.

"Here they come," said Marjorie, pointing towards the tribute band lugging heavy equipment up to the stage in preparation for their show. They seemed more subdued than usual, quietly going about their setup.

Perhaps they have been warned to behave.

After unpacking equipment and putting it in place, the men sat on the edge of the stage to watch the tail end of the volleyball game. The crew beat the officers by a considerable margin and Rachel wondered whether it could be a setup as a team building boost. The passengers applauded vigorously before filing back into the pool themselves and continuing with their own entertainment.

Jason spoke to Gordon for a short time while the band tuned their instruments to suit the open air surroundings.

"I wonder what Jason's speaking to Gordon about?"

"By the way he's just patted him on the shoulder, I would say he's offering his condolences," said Marjorie. "Here's a waiter, Rachel, would you like a drink?"

They ordered mocktails and scrutinised the band closely. "This is frustrating," said Rachel. "We need to get to meet them somehow – it's alright watching, but we need to speak to them."

"Consider it done, my dear. They will be joining us after their show."

"What? Why – how?" Rachel stared open-mouthed.

"I spoke to their agent while you phoned Sarah after lunch and told him you were a huge Queen fan and that I am thinking of hiring them for your birthday later in the year. I told him I needed you to meet them to make sure they would be suitable and that we would be attending this performance to check them out. I used my title during the introduction, of course – it does come in handy occasionally!"

Rachel gawped, shaking her head admiringly. "Lady Marjorie Snellthorpe, you have to be the most sharp-witted and devious woman I've ever met. I would never have thought of that."

"Decades of experience as the wife of an international businessman do come with some knowledge of how things work. Titles and money still go a long way, you know." Marjorie sniggered and the glint in her eye belied the piercingly sharp mind that accompanied it. A usually humble and unassuming woman, Marjorie rarely brought attention to her wealth or her title, but in this instance, Rachel was pleased she'd used both to full advantage.

"As long as they don't ask me too many questions about Queen or the game's up. Way before my time! My knowledge is limited to what I've read and what my father told me."

"I'm sure you'll ad lib marvellously. Anyway, they don't seem the enquiring type."

They laughed and enjoyed their drinks while waiting for the show to finish. Rachel felt glad when the band concluded as she reluctantly conceded they were not nearly as entertaining without the late Dominic Venables.

Jimmy, the manager, suddenly appeared at the side of the stage during the final song of the session. Mute applause followed from passengers who were not bathing or swimming in the pools as the lead guitarist and stand-in lead singer stormed off the stage and disappeared. Rachel observed Jimmy gather the rest of the band together after they had packed up their kit and escort them over to Rachel and Marjorie's table.

Marjorie stood, shook Jimmy's hand and introduced him to Rachel. Still battling with his gum from this morning, or perhaps having taken on a new piece, he shook Rachel's hand too.

"Ello, good to meet ya, Rachel. These are my boys, Dalton Delacruz aka John Deacon and Ray Lynch aka Roger Taylor. Nick's just gone to collect something from his room."

"No 'e's not," said Ray. "'E's got the 'ump cos no-one paid 'im much attention. I told 'im people just like a bit of background music, but you know 'ow 'e is. Mardy if 'e finks people ain't listening to 'im."

"I see, well, how do you do? I am Lady Marjorie Snellthorpe." Emphasis on *lady,* Rachel noticed. "And this is my granddaughter Rachel, who appreciated your performance."

The *boys*, as Jimmy had called them, grinned from ear to ear at this last part and nodded a greeting. They exchanged cursory looks as if not knowing what to do next.

"Please take a seat, gentlemen. Can I order you some drinks? You must be thirsty after that riveting performance."

Ray and Jimmy's enthusiasm went up a notch as Marjorie caught the attention of a waiter and ordered beers for the men and lemonade for herself and Rachel.

"I told the boys you might want us to do a gig for Rachel's birfday," said Jimmy. "You like Queen, then, do ya?" He glanced briefly at Rachel, but thankfully didn't wait for an answer, instead continuing to address Marjorie. "Can't say they were my cup o' tea, but the boys do a good job. As I said, Lady Snellforpe, they don't come cheap."

"Quite," said Marjorie. "Money isn't the issue here, but I would like to know more about who it is I'm hiring. I will need to meet, erm, Nick did you say? And the other band member – the one you mentioned the other night, Rachel. I think you said there were four?"

Rachel admired the way Marjorie had cut straight to the chase and dispensed with the blarney.

"Yes, a Freddie Mercury lookalike – a great singer," said Rachel on cue.

Nick arrived and caught the last part of the conversation. "Well, he won't be coming. Didn't you hear? He ended up in the drink. Singing with the angels now, or more than likely down there—" He pointed to the ground, smirking.

"Oh dear, how frightful! That must have been a terrible shock." Marjorie feigned horror.

"It must be hard for you to go on, I'm amazed you managed to sing so cheerfully," added Rachel beginning to enjoy the role play.

"To be honest, luv, he wasn't that good, and a right pain in the bum," said Nick dismissively, shrugging as he launched himself into a chair and lolled back casually.

"Creative temperament, you know the type," interjected Jimmy, chewing ever harder on his gum. His jaws tightened as they worked overtime, causing his saggy jowls to wobble in rhythm.

"I can't say that I do," said Marjorie. "What happened to the poor man?"

Cleverly, Rachel thought, Marjorie addressed her question to Dalton. Despite this, Nick answered while Dalton looked down at his shoes.

"No-one knows, he apparently fell overboard and hit his bonce. The doctors tried to save him, but he died in hospital in Copenhagen."

"That security geezer don't fink 'e fell. 'E finks 'e got pushed," said Ray, the drummer.

"Why would anyone want to push him overboard?" pressed Rachel before Jimmy could change the subject.

"Loads of reasons, luv," said Nick who looked her up and down appreciatively before continuing. "He always got someone's back up, argumentative plonker. If he wasn't arguing with someone, he would be seducing someone's bird."

"Now, now, Nick. Let's not speak ill of the dead," said Jimmy, chewing even more vigorously.

"But surely he wouldn't have had time to meet any women on board this ship to steal? We've only been at sea a few days."

"Don't you believe it," said Ray. "Dom worked fast and furious. As well as stealing birds, 'e always fell out with Nick 'ere. They 'ad a blazing row the night before 'e died."

"What are you implying?" Nick's face reddened and he looked ready to explode. "I didn't kill him. You had just as much reason to give him one after what he did to you and Jade."

Rachel inwardly smiled as this was all going to plan. The more they argued, the more they revealed and possible motives sprang to light.

"His brother had just as much reason to do him in." Dalton spoke so quietly the others didn't hear him as they continued to talk over each other, but Rachel heard.

"What makes you say that?" she prodded as he stared at his shoes again. He looked unsure, but she gave him one of her sweetest smiles, causing him to look up.

"Dom was knocking off his wife."

The men had quietened for a moment and caught Dalton's revelation.

"Whose wife?" asked Jimmy.

"Gordon's," answered Dalton.

Looks of genuine astonishment filled their faces. "You're kidding – no way," said Nick, open-mouthed. "That's the lowest of the low. How come you knew and we didn't? Are you making stuff up again?"

"Dalton's got a vivid imagination," interjected Jimmy. "Sometimes 'e's prone to embellishing the truf."

"No I'm not, I saw them. I took a walk in the early hours, the day he was killed. They were by the crew pool kissing in the shadows. I only noticed them cos a huge wave caused the ship to lurch. I caught them in a shaft of moonlight. I remember thinking the gleaming light could have been a spotlight on stage. They didn't notice me, though, too hard at it."

"Where was Gordon?" asked Ray.

"Working – I bumped into him soon after, heading out towards the pool, so I scarpered."

"Nice story, Dalton, but I saw Dom go to bed at one after I'd had my head glued. He was in no state to go prancing around the crew pool, I can tell you."

Dalton shook his head, tightened his lips and sulked, staring down at his shoes again.

Undeterred, Nick continued. "It could just as well have been Jimmy here. Hardly best buddies, were you?"

Jimmy looked decidedly uncomfortable about this revelation and the jaw burst into overdrive. If it had been a helicopter, he would have taken off. After chewing the gum into submission, he glared at Nick before looking at Marjorie pleadingly.

"Now, about this gig, ladies." He had clearly had enough of the direction the conversation had taken and was keen to get it back to its original purpose. "We will be back to being a band of four tomorrow, we've got an old band mate joining us in Tallinn, flown over specially."

"Yeah, and it's a good job he wasn't on board or he would have been the prime suspect," Nick threw in while facing off with Jimmy, clearly annoyed at being cut off in his prime.

Marjorie didn't pursue the subject and managed to defer her decision, dissipating the testosterone build up.

"We will need to meet again when your new man has settled in. We will attend a performance or two, and if Rachel likes what she sees, we will speak further. If I do hire you, it will be worth your while." The hint of generous remuneration caused Jimmy's eyes to light up. "There will be many wealthy guests at Rachel's party who could well follow up with invitations of their own. We are always looking for good acts for our circle of friends in London, not to mention the wealthy businessmen we entertain from all over the world."

Rachel knew she was being honest about everything, except a desire to hire this unruly bunch.

The men pushed their chairs back and rose to leave. Jimmy shook Marjorie's hand, obviously thinking they had the deal in the bag.

While Jimmy ingratiated himself sickeningly with Marjorie, Rachel spotted Waverley on the far side of the pool, scowling at them.

Whoops.

The group left and Marjorie looked triumphant.

"Wasn't that enlightening?"

"Yes, but look who's heading our way," said Rachel, inclining her head. Waverley was now marching towards them, having waited for the band to leave, and his face said it all. Clearly exasperated, he was struggling to keep his body language relaxed, but the red neck gave him away, as did the cough.

"Good afternoon, ladies. May I join you?" he said, smiling at a few passengers as they passed by.

"Chief Waverley, what a pleasant surprise," said Marjorie.

"We are just about to meet Sarah for afternoon tea in Creams," said Rachel. "Why don't you join us there?" She gave him enough eye contact to tell him they had information to share, but in a more private setting.

He got it immediately. Coughing, he replied, "I'll meet you there in twenty minutes."

Chapter 9

"If I see one more guy from that stag do, I'm going to jump overboard." Bernard flopped down on a chair in Gwen's office and let out a deep sigh. "Why couldn't they settle for a night out in Cardiff? No, obviously not good enough, so they decide to terrorise medical staff on a cruise ship. Well, I've had enough of them."

"It's not only us they're bothering," said Graham. "Those poor cheerleaders are sick of them too, not to mention the security team."

"Come on, you two bah humbugs. We were all young once," said Gwen.

"I was never that young," laughed Graham. "And I wouldn't have been able to afford a cruise for a stag do either."

"I can't afford a cruise now. If I didn't work on this ship, I wouldn't know they existed," moaned Bernard.

"Then be thankful and stop complaining," said Gwen.

Undeterred, Bernard looked at Sarah. "What do you think about them, Sarah?"

Sarah, still suffering from the loss of her childhood pet, answered absentmindedly. "They are boisterous, but they seem pretty harmless on the whole, I guess." Gwen looked sympathetic as Sarah had told her about Pickles when she'd asked her if anything was wrong this morning, noticing her eyes were swollen.

"Harmless?" chirped Brigitte. "I would like to give them all a good bit of French discipline."

"Not Madame Guillotine, I hope." Graham laughed. Brigitte scowled at him.

"Don't joke about such things. I am not proud of parts of French history, but you British have no room to talk."

"Sorry, no offence, and I agree those boys need a firm hand. Waverley will clamp down on them soon, I'm sure, and then they'll realise what discipline is."

They all laughed at this point. The medical team enjoyed their camaraderie and generally hit it off together. Bernard was the funny guy and usually made people happy, Brigitte could be blunt but was a pussycat underneath, Gwen, their team leader, reined them in when necessary and Sarah often provided the balance. Graham was the senior medical officer and liked to banter, but was well respected both in and out of the medical centre for his expertise and his poise in times of crisis.

Sarah looked around and noticed that the junior doctor was missing.

"Where's Alex?"

"He said he was going to check on the excursion staff to make sure they were all up-to-date with their medicals," said Graham. "I can't see why he didn't just check on the computer, but maybe he needed to stretch his legs."

The rest of the team shared some eyebrow raising and a joint smirk. "Yes, it's very important to stretch one's legs," laughed Bernard.

"What have I missed this time?" groaned Graham while draining his coffee cup.

"You'd better ask Alex. That's none of our concern," said Gwen, giving Bernard a warning look. "Haven't you got somewhere to be, Bernard?"

"Yes ma'am." He saluted and skulked out of the office.

"I'm going for lunch before taking a nap. I was up all night last night. Are you coming for lunch, Sarah?" asked Brigitte.

"Yes, anyone else?"

"I'll take a rain check on that one, I need to write some reports," answered Gwen.

"Me too. I'm meeting with Richard to discuss budgets – believe me, I'd much rather be with you."

Graham met regularly with the ship's administrator to justify current spending and put in bids for new equipment when they needed it. Sarah smiled sympathetically and followed Brigitte out of the medical centre.

Brigitte headed back to her room after lunch and Sarah wandered around the ship's library, choosing a light-hearted chick-lit book. Afterwards she made her way to the crew pool, armed with her reading material. The pool area was relatively quiet as most of the crew were at work or catching up on sleep. There was a group of Romanian barmen she recognised throwing a floating disc to each other in the pool, splashing about happily. They waved to acknowledge her and then carried on with their game.

Sarah walked over to a quieter side of the crew area where she found Gordon standing in the shadows of an alcove, staring at the wall.

"Hello, Gordon."

He almost leapt out of his skin before recovering himself. "Hello," he answered glumly.

"I'm so sorry about your brother."

"Not half as sorry as I am about my brother." His eyes flamed as he spat the words out with such venom, Sarah automatically took a step back.

"Perhaps you'd rather be alone," she said, hoping he would say yes. There was way too much testosterone floating round this ship for her liking.

"No, it's okay. It might be nice to have someone to talk to. Shall we sit over there?" He pointed to a table overlooking the sea. Sarah sighed, but reluctantly followed. They sat in silence while Sarah struggled, not knowing what to say.

"Have security said any more about how he died?"

In for a penny.

"They're not saying too much, but they reckon someone hit him over the head and threw him overboard. At first they said he might have fallen after drinking too much, but now they're saying it's suspicious. My parents are distraught – he's always been the bee's knees." The bitterness in his tone was clearly historical. "Anyway, they've flown over to Copenhagen with my sister to wait for the coroner to release him."

"I'm sure you could ask for compassionate leave, you know."

"To do what?" he snapped. "Join my parents crooning over their beloved favourite son? No thanks, I'd rather work." His eyes filled with tears, but the hatred emanating from them unnerved her.

"At least you've got Shirley on board. I'm sure she'll help you get through this."

He raised his voice several decibels. "OH YES, AT LEAST I'VE GOT HER!" He glared out to sea.

One of the Romanian barmen left the pool and came over. "Nurse, you alright?"

"Yes, I'm okay, thank you."

The man didn't leave. He stared at Gordon. "Come join us in the pool, man."

"No, I need to get back to work." Gordon pushed the chair back with such ferocity it fell over and stormed off.

"Sorry for interrupting, Nurse, but I didn't want to leave you with him. He behaving weird. And between you and me, he hated brother."

"Really? Why?"

"Not sure, but one of barmen heard them arguing. Not normal argue. He threaten to kill brother, and now look."

"Have you spoken to the security team about this?"

"No, they never speak to us. We not important, but you always kind to us so I not leaving you with him."

"Well, thank you, and I'll tell the security chief what you've said. It might be important."

"Okay, they know where we are if they need speak with us."

Sarah nodded, thanking him again for coming to her rescue before she made her way to Creams to meet Rachel and Marjorie for tea.

Chapter 10

Waverley arrived at the same time as Sarah, much to Rachel's disappointment. She had wanted to check her friend was alright after the previous night as they had not had time to talk properly when Rachel called to arrange the meet up.

"He doesn't look too happy," Marjorie chuckled.

"I suppose he imagines we've been snooping," giggled Rachel.

"What's so funny?" asked Sarah, who hadn't noticed Waverley coming up behind her. She joined them at the corner table they had deliberately chosen for its privacy.

"Marjorie was just telling me something funny." Rachel nodded, moving her eyes towards Waverley, telepathically signalling to Sarah not to ask any further questions.

Waverley hovered over the table, looking decidedly uncomfortable with a frown plastered on his face.

"Oh, do sit down, man," ordered Marjorie, to which he obediently responded, taking the fourth chair at the table.

"Well, as long as you don't mind me intruding on your tea. I do need to speak to you all if it's convenient."

Sarah appeared confused. Marjorie was in her element.

"You can speak to us all you like once we've ordered tea."

Waverley coughed. "Yes, of course."

The waiter saved him further embarrassment by appearing at the table, notebook in hand. They ordered tea and pastries. Waverley, more reluctantly than the rest of them, finally placed an order for coffee and a cookie under the watchful gaze of Marjorie.

"How was your morning?" Rachel asked Sarah.

"Busy as ever. The stag party continues to cause havoc, much to Bernard's disgust. He's getting tired of them."

"What have they done now?" asked Waverley.

"Nothing major – they're just injury prone, that's all. You know how young people are – they never look where they're going."

"You're not so old yourself, dear," said Marjorie kindly. She had heard about Sarah's cat and sympathised when Rachel told her, being an animal lover herself.

"I feel much older when up against them. It must be nursing – we grow up fast, and there is a four year age difference, which seemingly accounts for a lot in your twenties."

"Oh listen to Old Mother Time!" Rachel teased.

Sarah laughed. "I'm a bit of a grouch when it comes to boys behaving badly."

"I expect they would have fewer accidents if they drank less," remarked Waverley. "I envisage a couple of them being under house arrest before long. It doesn't help that the cheerleaders continue to mix with them, in spite of complaining about their behaviour. What are we supposed to do? My team is stretched to the limit trying to keep them in check, and at the same time, investigate an apparent murder."

All eyes turned to Waverley as the drinks and food were delivered to their table. Once the waiter had gone, Marjorie said what everyone was thinking.

"You've confirmed it was murder then?"

"Yes, either that or manslaughter. The coroner suggests from the evidence that the man was unconscious when he hit the water. The scans show no fluid in the nasal cavities, which is apparently significant. That and the witness statements we sent through to her confirm he didn't struggle for breath. She says that the bruise to Mr Venables's head was caused by trauma from a blunt instrument and there was a cut from whatever was used to hit him. The blow to the head caused a catastrophic haemorrhage to the brain fairly soon afterwards."

"But you brought him round, didn't you, Sarah?" said Rachel.

"Not me alone, the team did, but the bleed may have been a slow-burner followed by a rupture. It's not uncommon if the blow was particularly hard or if the person had an undiagnosed aneurysm."

"That's what the coroner says," said Waverley, admiring Sarah's explanation.

"So someone did hit him. I don't suppose it could have been a bang to the head following a fall?" asked Rachel.

"Not according to the coroner."

"Any idea who might have hit him?"

"Any number of people are in the frame for that." Waverley shrugged his shoulders and his drooping head and furrowed brow betrayed his worry and exasperation. "I can't get much information out of anyone. None of the band seems to have sensible alibis for the time of death, but they insist they all got on and were good friends."

Marjorie guffawed and Rachel laughed out loud, partly at Marjorie and partly because of the astonishment on Waverley's face at her outburst.

"Come on, you two. You've obviously discovered something, so out with it," said Sarah, looking sympathetically at Waverley.

Rachel explained about Marjorie's subterfuge and how the ruse had caused the men to join them after their performance on the lido deck.

"Very noisy it was too," interjected Marjorie. "Rachel says they weren't nearly as good without their lead singer."

Waverley stifled a tut as his impatience became visible at the interruption, but controlled himself and encouraged Rachel to continue with the story.

Once Rachel had explained how none of the band or even the manager seemed to have liked Dominic Venables and how they were all overly eager to point the finger at each other, Waverley sat back in his chair, confused.

"It doesn't change anything, I'm no nearer to knowing who hit him," he said.

"One of them could be lying, or maybe all of them. They seem to be doing a reverse alibi thing to make you work harder, and they probably find it amusing. I wouldn't trust them with a dime, as my husband used to say." Marjorie had a point. The tribute band members were the least likeable group of people Rachel had met in a long time. "And I wouldn't rule that shifty manager out, either," Marjorie added.

"I agree," said Rachel. "The way he chews that gum strikes me as overly aggressive. I have a gut feeling about him."

"Oh no, not your gut feelings!" Waverley almost smiled as he groaned. Rachel had got to the bottom of two cases of murder on her previous cruises on board the *Coral Queen* aided by her gut.

"There is something else," added Rachel. "One of the group, the one called

Dalton, said that Dominic Venables was having an affair with his brother Gordon's wife. Gordon's the new cruise director."

"I'm well aware who Gordon is," snapped Waverley, immediately apologising for his outburst.

"The others didn't seem to know about the affair and scoffed at him – apparently Dalton is known for making things up or embellishing the truth, but he was pretty adamant that he saw them kissing at the side of the crew pool in the early hours before Venables was killed. He also says he bumped into Gordon heading that way afterwards."

"Do you believe him?" asked Waverley.

"He seemed sincere. He's much quieter than the others. He may have exaggerated the story, but I can't see why he'd make it up. Apparently Dom was a renowned philanderer—"

"That would explain Gordon's anger, if he did catch them out," Sarah interrupted.

"What do you mean, Sarah?" asked Waverley, gulping back his coffee and almost choking.

"Just before I came here, I found him in the crew area by the pool. He looked distraught, so I tried to comfort him, but he soon became vehemently angry. I would say the hatred in his eyes was caused by something other than his brother's death. It also sounded like their parents favoured Dom, and Gordon's very bitter about that too, so it may have been a mixture of grief and anger. I'm not saying he murdered his brother, which would be awful, but he didn't like him, and he did become enraged when I mentioned his wife."

"I noticed that anger in his eyes when Marjorie and I saw him in the Sky View Lounge. People do react differently to the death of a loved one, though, and we can't be certain the wife was having an affair. It might be sibling rivalry and now Gordon feels guilty because he hated his brother. But didn't you say Gordon got the band the job in the first place?"

"That's what I heard from Rosa Doherty. We got talking when I went to treat one of the dancers who had an ankle injury. Two of the band passed by and she muttered under her breath. I later asked her what that was all about and she told me she had made a mistake hiring them and shouldn't have allowed Gordon to persuade her to."

"So now we have at least five suspects, but do any of them fit the profile of a killer?" said Waverley. "Gordon has to be my chief suspect for now, judging by what you've just told me."

"If he deliberately got his brother on board, it could be premeditated murder," said Rachel thoughtfully.

"I realise you will find it difficult to stay out of this, Rachel, Lady Snellthorpe, but I would very much prefer it if you did—"

"Bah!" exclaimed Marjorie, interrupting Waverley. "Not going to happen, Chief, so we either club together, or Rachel and I find the killer for ourselves. We've found out a good deal of information for you so far."

Waverley answered tight lipped. "You stay with the band, I will speak to Gordon. Sarah, I shouldn't ask, but would you have a word with Shirley Venables? She might be more likely to open up to you as a nurse."

Sarah nodded. "I'll try. I can arrange a health promotion session for the dancers and quiz her. She's also due to see me about something else – confidential, so I can't go into it, but that might provide an opportunity. I'm sure I'll be able to wangle it somehow, but I'm not going to ask her if she was having an affair with her brother-in-law."

"I have no idea what my team are going to do with themselves while all these amateurs conduct enquiries," conceded Waverley.

"I do," said Sarah, nodding towards the public area outside the patisserie where a crowd of twenty youths were congregating.

"Ah, yes." Waverley smiled for the first time that afternoon. "Our delightful stag party."

"And the cheerleaders, of course," said Marjorie, laughing. "Whatever they are."

Rachel looked to see if she was teasing or whether she seriously had no knowledge of cheerleading. Marjorie was giving nothing away, but she winked as she sipped her tea, a pinkie in the air of course. Admiring her elderly friend's elegance and poise, Rachel smiled affectionately.

Chapter 11

Jack Waverley came away from the meeting with Rachel, Lady Snellthorpe and Sarah grinning smugly. Let them chase the band around as much as they liked, that should keep them out of mischief, or more importantly to him, danger. He had grown fond of Rachel and Lady Snellthorpe and didn't want either of them putting themselves at risk on board his ship. Security was his concern and Rachel had been lucky to escape with her life on two previous cruises. He didn't believe in tempting providence too often.

He felt certain the tribute act would turn out to have cast iron alibis and agreed with Rachel: they were giving him the run-around in that respect. Despite knowing that the band argued a lot, he felt sure that underneath it all, they tolerated each other for their mutual love of music, such as it was. According to a member of the crew working in the casino, they stuck up for each other when push came to shove. They had rooms on her deck and she heard them laughing a lot in between incessant arguments. She told him these creative types often behaved like that: volatile one minute, effusive and lovey dovey the next.

He would focus on Gordon for now, although he remained to be convinced about the affair. The couple seemed happy enough, and he liked Gordon, preferring him to Matt. The previous cruise director had been an arrogant, pig-headed man who tended to upset the crew. Word got back to Waverley about these things from Brenda, his girlfriend who worked in the bakery. She didn't miss a thing, and keeping up with the gossip helped him to keep the passengers and crew safe.

Maybe the time had come to tie the knot again. He'd been thinking about it for months now, but hadn't quite plucked up the courage to ask Brenda, ten years his junior – a matter which bothered him. His daughter, Charlotte, liked her and had thus far been encouraging about his new relationship. This pleased him because Charlotte remained especially close to her mother who'd left him for one of his closest friends.

Waverley knew all about betrayal, and if Gordon was suffering, he understood exactly what he might be going through. He had never known anger like it when he'd found out he had been betrayed by two of the people he loved the most, but even in his darkest days he had never contemplated murder. Nowadays he tolerated the couple for his daughter's sake, but they would never be friends again as long as he had breath.

Waverley made his way towards guest services to check the cruise director's itinerary. He could have phoned down, but needed the exercise, concerned about his recent weight gain. He tapped his abdomen subconsciously as he arrived at the desk and asked for the document he needed.

A constant queue of people was present at the guest services desk during sea days with multiple requests and complaints, from lights not working to rooms being too hot or too cold and everything in between. The guest services staff performed their duty in the well-briefed fashion that had been drummed into them to assist with every eventuality, and they did so admirably.

Waverley stood by one of the marble posts on deck four, observing the crowds for a few minutes while scanning the document in his hands. He had fifteen minutes before Gordon would finish hosting a couples' quiz in the Plato Lounge. That was only one floor up so he took the stairs and stood at the rear of the lounge until proceedings concluded.

Gordon was nowhere in sight. Geraldine, the assistant cruise director, seemed to be in full control of the event and looked as though she relished being the centre of attention, but not as much as Gordon appeared to enjoy it. Waverley would hate it. Being reserved and preferring privacy, he kept himself to himself wherever possible. It must run in the family for Gordon, he mused as he watched Geraldine finish off the session with a joke, resulting in raucous laughter from the assembled crowd of couples.

Before he got the opportunity to ask her where he could find Gordon, his radio burst into life.

"Yes, what is it?" Irritation came through in his voice after being halted in his tracks.

"Sorry, sir, a fight's broken out on the lido deck." Ravanos sounded breathless.

"On my way." Frustrated, he heaved his shoulders up, sighed heavily and walked briskly towards the lifts.

Chapter 12

After the meeting with Waverley, Marjorie went back to her room for a shower and to change for dinner. Rachel took the opportunity to spend some time with Sarah. They walked along the upper decks, enjoying the fresh air.

"How are you? You said you were okay, but how are you, really?"

"Actually, I am alright. I cried myself to sleep last night, but today, work has taken my mind off things. This morning, Gwen asked what was wrong because she could see I'd been crying. She has been kind and supportive. I suppose being away from home helps – I don't have the daily reminder of the empty cat bed or anything like that. I expect Mum will feel it more than I will for now."

They walked side by side, Sarah dressed in uniform with two-and-a-half gold stripes on her epaulettes signifying her officer status, and Rachel casually dressed in lime-green crop trousers and a white vest top. They stopped at the inner rail on deck fourteen, overlooking the pools on the lido deck and enjoyed a casual conversation. Out of the corner of her eye, Rachel noticed Dalton speaking quietly to a woman at the side of the stage. He stroked her arm before she headed away. Rachel felt pleased for him that he had found someone else on board other than his negative band mates.

Sarah was looking in the opposite direction, watching children splashing in the pools when a scream drew both of them out of their reverie. Rachel spun her head away from the stage to the side of the main pool where two men were fighting, one grasping the other in a headlock. A young woman, probably early twenties, was screaming and crying for them to stop. Crowds of onlookers gathered quickly, but no sign of security.

Rachel and Sarah raced down the stairs and pushed their way through the crowd with Sarah commanding people to stand back while radioing down for security.

"Make way, please."

The onlookers at the front of the crowd reluctantly stepped aside. By now, one man was on the floor, bleeding badly from his head, while the other one continued to pummel him. Rachel thought if she didn't act quickly, the aggressor might kill him, so she grabbed the man on the top from behind.

"Please, sir, leave him. He's had enough."

Rage spilled from the man, who she was shocked to see was Gordon. With uncontrolled anger, he struggled from

Rachel's grip, pushing her backwards, and jumped on the man again, leaving Rachel no choice. This time she was firm, arm locking him in a vice-like grip.

A few minutes later, Waverley and two other security guards, including Jason, arrived, taking over.

Sarah attended to the man on the ground. Calling for the on-call medic, she shouted to the waiters in the crowd.

"Someone get me the first aid kit and water. I need clean cloths too."

Rachel released Gordon so that Jason could handcuff him before leading him away.

"Get rid of these crowds," Waverley snarled at Ravanos, the other officer, who began gently ushering people back.

"Show's over, folks. Those who witnessed the incident from the beginning please take a seat and we will interview you shortly." He pointed to chairs under a canopy. "Otherwise, please clear the area. It will be open again as soon as the scene is cleared."

The inquisitive crowd moved slowly away, some muttering while others took seats as instructed. Many of the passengers, including those with children, had already left when the fight started.

"How is he?" Rachel handed Sarah water, a first aid kit and towels that had been brought by pool attendants.

"Pretty beaten up, but it looks worse than it is – faces always bleed badly. I'm not sure he would have been alright for much longer if you hadn't intervened, though."

"Who is he?"

"I'm not sure. I think he's one of the boys from the stag party."

"He is." A girl's blubbering came from nearby. "His name's Dave, he'll be the best man when Aled gets married."

Graham and Bernard arrived with the medical kit and helped Sarah stem the bleeding from Dave's face; he was now sitting up and mumbling to Sarah. Rachel recognised the situation was under control, so she led the girl away to one side and urged her to sit down.

"I'm Rachel, what's your name?"

"Tonya, I'm with a group of cheerleaders from Massachusetts. It was awful, I thought that crazy man was going to kill him. Doesn't he work on board?"

Ignoring the question, Rachel asked, "Why don't you start at the beginning and tell me what happened?"

They heard the sound of Waverley's cough before he appeared and introduced himself. Joining Rachel and Tonya, he handed them both a cup of tea.

"We were sitting by the pool having a laugh, that's all," said Tonya. "Dave was telling me how he'd caught one of the dancers snogging an older guy from a band on board ship. We were laughing about it when this guy, I'm sure he works on the ship, pulled him out of his seat and started yelling at him. Dave swore, told him to get a life, and the man punched him full in the face. I screamed, Dave fell over, just missing the pool, and the man leapt on him like a madman. He kept punching him. I shouted and cried, asking people to help – some ran away and others just watched. I even saw a couple of guys filming it on their mobile phones – how sick is that?"

Rachel put a hand on Tonya's arm as she continued to sob. By now the cheerleader was shaking.

"Did you recognise the men filming? Are they still here?" asked Waverley, handing her his lily-white handkerchief.

Tonya wiped her eyes and blew her nose, sniffing as she looked around. "That fat guy over there was one and the other one was older. He's not here now. He had long greying hair. He might have been in the band that played earlier."

Waverley looked confused and Rachel digested this information. Why would Ray Lynch be filming the fight?

The medical team were wheeling the shocked Dave away from the area.

"Can I go with him?" Tonya asked.

"Yes, of course, Miss," said Waverley. "Would you just give me your full name for my records in case I need to speak with you again?"

"Tonya Carson," the girl shouted as she ran after the medical team.

"Sounds like wrong place, wrong time to me," said Waverley.

"Obviously Gordon did know about the affair then if it was his wife they were referring to."

"Possibly, but it could have been any of the dancers – there are eighteen in the troupe and multitudes of older men on the ship. Gordon may have got the wrong end of the stick completely, idiot." Waverley shook his head in disbelief. "Now he's ruined his career, such as it was."

"What will happen to him?"

"He'll be put in the brig to cool off and then placed under house arrest. I'll have to interview him. If he wasn't a suspect in a murder investigation, I'd put him off in Tallinn in the morning, but as it is, I'm going to have to hang on to him as well as that rabble of a band. One of my officers will now be tied up babysitting outside his room until I get to the bottom of the murder of Dominic Venables. Gordon has just become my prime suspect, certainly has a temper from what that young lady told us. We'll need to see if the injured guy wants to press charges as well. Either

178

way, Gordon's in big trouble – the cruise line will pay to compensate the young man for his silence if he agrees, and they'll want rid of Venables. They can't have employees attacking passengers – this is a nightmare.

"Perhaps Gordon Venables is just as bad as his brother – I don't know how he came to us with glowing references. I'll be going through his security file with a fine toothcomb. The captain will speak to the powers that be and see what they are prepared to offer the boy for his silence. It's a complete and utter mess, and for what? All because he overheard a stupid conversation between a couple of kids."

Rachel felt sorry for the chief of security. "I'm not sure he murdered his brother."

"Dare I ask why?"

"Think about it: if you had just murdered someone, wouldn't you want to keep your head down rather than get embroiled in a fight with one of the passengers? I accept he's livid about his wife possibly having an affair with his brother, but the rest doesn't add up."

"Killing isn't logical, Rachel. These things do happen – perhaps he can't rationalise at the moment. I don't know, maybe he's looking for someone else to kill."

He and Rachel looked at each other, suddenly concerned for Gordon's wife's welfare. Waverley picked up his radio.

"Get me Rosa, pronto!" he yelled.

They held their breath and waited. Waverley's radio lit up and he answered.

"Rosa, I need to know if Shirley Venables is with you." His shoulders relaxed. "Thank you. No, nothing at present, I'll talk to you later." He turned to Rachel. "She's in a dress rehearsal, been there most of the afternoon."

"Thank goodness for that," replied Rachel.

He stood up. "Thanks for what you did, you prevented a nasty situation becoming much more serious." He coughed, embarrassed. "Anyway, I need to go and interview the 'would be' filmmaker before the footage makes its way on to YouTube or CNN. I suppose you're coming?"

Sarah had left with the medical team so Rachel gladly followed Waverley over to where a bariatric young man was seated, looking at the mobile held in chubby, short-fingered hands.

"Good afternoon, sir," said Waverley. "I'm Chief Security Officer Waverley. This is Rachel Prince who broke up the fight I believe you witnessed. I understand you have mobile phone footage of the incident?"

"I sure do, Officer Waverley." The man had an American drawl. "Nasty incident it was too. Your security needs tightening up if you ask me."

Waverley's neck reddened. "May I see the footage?"

The man looked unsure, holding his phone tightly in his hand. "Well, I don't know about that. This is my personal property. I could sell this film to a news station, show them what goes on aboard your cruise ship."

Waverley's neck became a deeper red and his temple veins pulsated as he tensed. "Sir, maritime law applies to what happens on board a ship, and you are in possession of evidence I need. I either confiscate the phone or you show me the footage."

The man sighed deeply, his bulging grey eyes darting around. Rachel noticed he had no eyebrows and looked fearful of something. He reluctantly handed the phone over to Waverley.

"Just that video, mind," he said as Waverley prised the phone from his tightened hand.

Waverley looked at the screen, raised his eyebrows, scrunching up his face as he scrolled back to the beginning of the video. He held the phone so Rachel was able see. The film footage revealed why the young man was so possessive of his phone. It started with close ups of various women in bikinis before zooming in on buttocks and cleavages. Rachel frowned while Waverley looked at the man in disgust. The film swung round as a commotion occurred and showed the young guy Dave falling to the ground and Gordon going for him like a man possessed.

When they'd finished watching the film, the man held his hand out. Waverley leaned forward.

"Sir, I will be confiscating this phone as evidence and need your permission to copy the relevant footage."

"You can't do that! I refuse, and I need that phone."

"In that case, I'll show this and any other videos found on the device to the authorities when we arrive in Tallinn – where they have different laws to us – if that's what you prefer?"

"No, no – you can hang on to it and delete the video off the phone when you're done, as long as that's the last I hear of it. I haven't broken the law." The man was red and sweating.

"Name?"

"Arnold Blake."

"Room number?"

"9065, sir."

Waverley wrote the details down. "You can come to my office on disembarkation day and collect your phone, Mr Blake. My security officers will be following you closely. I suggest you make sure the only films recorded on any device from here on in consist of scenery. If I find anything illegal on this or any other device, I will report it to the relevant authorities. Do we understand each other?"

"Yes, sir. There's nothing illegal. I just like to admire – you know." His head dropped.

"You may go."

Arnold Blake heaved his enormous frame from the chair with some difficulty, but Waverley offered no assistance. Once he'd gone, Waverley let rip.

"Pervert! I'd like to put him in the brig if I thought he'd fit."

"Nasty piece of work, but I guess he doesn't have much luck with women. He might have health issues and his weight has nothing to do with his behaviour."

"I disagree, Rachel – it has everything to do with his weight. If he wasn't built like that, he wouldn't need to film women, would he?"

"Don't be ridiculous, you're showing your prejudice. I arrest perverts at least once a month and they come in all shapes and sizes. If it were that simple, I should arrest everyone over a certain weight, according to you."

Waverley looked suitably rebuked. "I don't like this sort of thing, that's all – if he'd been skinny, I'd have probably been personal about that, too. Sorry." He thrust the phone in his pocket. "I'd better help Ravanos interview the rest of this crowd. I'll talk to you and Sarah later."

He got up and headed towards half a dozen passengers still waiting to be interviewed. Rachel returned to her room to change for dinner.

Chapter 13

At breakfast the next morning, Rachel noticed Marjorie seemed off colour.

"Are you alright? You don't seem yourself."

"To be honest, I don't feel well. I have a migraine coming on. Do you mind if I stay on board today? Perhaps all the excitement has been a bit too much."

Rachel felt guilty for having allowed them to become embroiled in an investigation which strictly speaking had nothing to do with them.

"I don't mind at all. I'll stay with you."

"No, dear, there's really no need. I have Migraleve tablets with me, I'll take some and go back to bed. Once they kick in, I'll be better – it will be gone by this evening. Anyway, you're meeting Sarah. That girl doesn't get much time off – you must go."

Rachel considered it for a moment. Not wanting to disappoint Sarah but not wanting to leave Marjorie by herself if she was unwell, she was torn. However, seeing the determination in the old lady's eyes and knowing how independent and stubborn Marjorie could be, she opted not to argue.

"As long as I can escort you back to your room and ask Mario to check in on you while I'm out."

"That would be acceptable," Marjorie conceded.

Once she had settled Marjorie into bed, clucking like a mother hen, as her dear old friend chided, Rachel went downstairs to meet Sarah in the main atrium. While sitting at a table waiting, she watched people coming and going, preparing for their various outings. One of the luxuries of cruising was the excitement of waking up every morning in a different place or country and leaving the ship to go exploring.

She heard arguing coming from a nearby table and noticed the tribute band members once again having a heated discussion. A few women were with them, being just as loud as the men. Rachel sighed, thinking how tiresome they were.

They fell silent when Waverley approached. He said a few words then sat down. The conversation was now too quiet for Rachel to hear, but Waverley looked outwardly calm at least.

I wonder if he's quizzing Ray about filming the fight.

A couple approached the band's table from behind Waverley, but when they saw him, they turned and walked away. Rachel watched them meander round the customer services area looking at papers, but now and then they would surreptitiously glance over to the table where Waverley was seated.

Curious, she thought. She took out her phone and pretended to read from the screen while snapping a photo of the couple, whom she hadn't seen before, and then a short video of their behaviour. They whispered to each other before rushing off downstairs, presumably to vacate the ship.

Sarah finally arrived, wearing mufti for the land outing. Her eyes were still slightly swollen, suggesting she had likely cried again last night over Pickles. Rachel stood and hugged her, squeezing her arm at the same time.

"Where's Marjorie?"

"She's got a migraine, so she's gone back to bed."

"Oh dear, does she need any tablets?"

"No, she's brought her own along with her and has taken two. I did offer to stay, but she said she'd rather sleep it off. Mario's going to check in on her at lunchtime." Rachel noticed out of the corner of her eye the band heading downstairs. "How are you?"

"Better, thanks. Still sad, but I don't get that much time to think. It is for the best – I wouldn't want him to suffer, and he had a long life."

"Miss Prince, Nurse Bradshaw." Waverley spotted them and Rachel detected a note of irritation in his formal address.

"What have we done this time?" she whispered to Sarah.

"Pardon?" said Waverly.

"I said, 'Is that the time?' We're taking a trip today."

"Hmm." He knew she'd said something completely different, but didn't pursue it. "I've just been speaking to members of that tribute band. Funny how you're always around when I'm carrying out my enquiries."

"Sarcasm doesn't become you, and for your information, I was waiting for Sarah, who has just arrived. Yesterday, you gave me and Marjorie permission to speak to the men in the band – not that we've had any more opportunities with all the other goings on."

"In that case, I apologise. Have a good day, ladies." He marched off towards the rear stairs.

"He's insufferable sometimes. Yesterday we were included and today he's giving nothing away."

"Perhaps as well, Rachel. He can see your cogs turning as well as I can. He knows you won't let it go, but what say we go and join our tour before we miss the bus?"

Sarah laughed. She did seem brighter.

Not totally put off, Rachel continued while they walked down a deck to the exit.

"Waverley was talking to the band and some women with them in hushed tones. I expect he was asking about Ray filming the fight yesterday. In spite of what he says, they have to be high on his list of suspects, along with Gordon. I also spotted a couple I've not seen before behaving suspiciously when Waverley was with the group."

"Oh no," Sarah groaned. "You're not going to stop until you've got to the bottom of this, are you?"

Rachel grinned, and then turned serious. "To be honest, I am having second thoughts. I don't want all the excitement to make Marjorie ill – I forget sometimes just how old she is."

"I'm above telling you I told you so, but I did."

Rachel took her friend's arm. "I know. On a different subject, how's that young man, Dave?"

"He was kept in the infirmary overnight as a precaution. Graham needed to ensure there were no complications from the battering to his head. I suspect he also wanted to make sure news of the attack didn't spread like wildfire. His name's Dave Hughes and he's going to be the best man at the forthcoming wedding. He organised the stag do, I discovered. He needed some glue to his forehead and I'm sure he'll have a black eye this morning, but other than that, he'll recover. He even joked later on that he'd had worse on the rugby pitch."

"That explains his nose shape," said Rachel. "I thought it looked like it had been broken."

"Yes it has, but not yesterday, thankfully. That young cheerleader stayed with him for a few hours before rejoining her friends."

"Tonya," said Rachel, absentmindedly. "Do you imagine he'll sue?"

"I doubt it. The cruise line offers generous compensation for injuries aboard and they'll want to settle out of court if it comes to it."

They passed through security and found the group they would be with for their tour milling around at the side of the dock.

"That's Gordon's wife," said Sarah, "with the group over there."

Rachel recognised some of the dancers from the performance she had watched with Marjorie last night. Sarah had worked the previous evening, so Rachel and Marjorie had met up with Ron and Mabel, the elderly couple from Texas, and gone to the theatre together.

"Which one is she?"

"The one with the black bob."

Rachel saw a pretty woman, about the same height as her, wearing yellow cotton trousers and a tight fitting patterned vest with yellow speckles. She stood tall and straight and was wearing sunglasses that disguised her eyes.

"She doesn't seem the type to be snogging her brother-in-law."

"Pray tell me, what does the type look like?"

"Good point." Rachel chuckled. "Not like her, though. I wonder if Dalton is making it up."

"If that's the case, why would Gordon have attacked Dave yesterday?"

"I'm keeping an open mind. We need to talk to her."

Sarah put her arm through Rachel's and led her towards the coach that was now boarding.

"So much for my nice day out," she sighed.

They found two seats, Rachel keeping one eye on the dancers, paying particular attention to Shirley Venables. Sarah nudged her, giving her a disparaging glare.

The tour leader introduced herself before describing the highlights of the tour as the coach made its way out of the port and off to its destination. Rachel sat back.

"Sorry. You're right. Let's just have a nice outing."

Sarah smiled back, but her eyes said she wasn't convinced for one moment, and Rachel knew her friend was right.

They meandered along cobbled streets, taking in the sights and sounds of a new country. Sarah had an SLR camera with her, being an amateur photographer, and stopped whenever the opportunity to exercise her creative skills presented itself. Rachel didn't mind; she was pleased to see her friend happy and was well aware of how hard Sarah worked as a cruise ship nurse. It was important for her to have some down time as a tourist herself.

The streets were idyllic, or would have been if they weren't packed with cruise passengers. The locals were friendly and welcoming – the tour guide had explained that tourism was an important source of their income.

"Rachel, sit on that wall," Sarah directed, having spotted an attractive fountain with a church entrance in the field of vision behind. The sun was sending speckles of light through the leaves of a large willow tree to their left, and even Rachel recognised the ideal photo opportunity. She finally settled into the right position after numerous attempts that weren't quite right for her friend's eagle eye.

"I'm beginning to realise how a bride must feel on their wedding day!" Rachel rolled her eyes as she had to make yet another adjustment – her bag wasn't in the right place for Sarah, aka David Bailey.

"You still owe me for making me break every rule in the book on the last cruise, so don't you dare moan!"

"Now you're lowering yourself to emotional blackmail." Rachel laughed.

"Like you didn't use that as well!"

"Okay, you win. I know when to quit, just get it over with so we can have some lunch. I'm starving."

Sarah was right: Rachel had led her friend astray during her last cruise and put Sarah at risk of losing her job, something she had regretted immediately afterwards.

They bantered some more while Sarah took a range of casual photos. Just as she was about to put the camera away, the dancing group walked up the hill behind her.

"Would you mind taking a photo of the two of us?" called Rachel, making eye contact with the woman Sarah had identified earlier as Shirley Venables. Sarah shot her a warning glance. "What? It will be nice to have a photo together."

Sarah's eyebrows headed towards the sky as Shirley stepped away from the crowd.

"Sure, I'd be happy to," she said.

Funny, Rachel had presumed she was English, but the accent was German. Rather than trying to teach Shirley how to use the SLR, Sarah handed her a mobile phone to take the picture with, and then joined Rachel on the wall. The others in the crowd stopped and waited.

"Don't worry," said Shirley. "I'll catch up with you." They gladly walked on, laughing and joking after nodding or saying hello to Sarah.

After taking a couple of photos and showing the results to Sarah for approval, Shirley handed over her own mobile phone so Rachel could take a photo of her by the fountain. Rachel couldn't resist the temptation to take a quick scroll through Shirley's other photos once she had snapped a couple, while Sarah chatted amicably with the woman. After the photo shoot, they all headed in the direction the other dancers had taken.

The dance troupe had stopped at an outside café. Shirley rejoined her group.

Rachel nudged Sarah and mouthed, "Appointment!"

Sarah shook her head before leading Rachel away.

"Come on, Sherlock, let's get some food inside you."

"Did she say anything important?" Rachel asked.

"Yes, she told me her life story, and then confessed to having an affair and to her husband killing his brother – case solved, all in the three seconds we had!"

"You know, sarcasm doesn't suit you – you've been spending too much time with Brigitte," Rachel giggled.

They walked arm in arm down the cobbled road, laughing and joking until they found another café where they sat at an outside table and studied the menu.

"Right, seeing as you've dragged me away from our investigation, what do you recommend that's traditionally Estonian?"

Sarah gawped. "Our investigation? There's no 'our' about it." Her eyes caught Rachel's teasing smirk and she burst out laughing.

"I'll tell you what I found on the mobile phone after lunch."

"Rachel Prince – you didn't? Well don't tell me anything at the moment, I'm too hungry. We must have walked for miles. My feet are killing me."

"Well you will wear DCs when walking through cobbled streets."

Sarah looked down at her feet. Although her shoes were lovely, the soles were not suitable for the type of walking they had been doing.

"Okay, Miss Practicality, I wondered why you were wearing sturdy shoes on such a hot day. How was I to know you were going to drag me round every street in Tallinn? We are supposed to be on a bus tour."

"Yep, a bus tour marked as including moderate exercise, the brochure said."

Sarah picked up the menu and chewed her bottom lip as she did when she was concentrating. Rachel was delighted her friend was back to her normal bubbly self.

"So what do you recommend?"

"The last time I was here, I had a traditional dish with anchovies."

"Okay, anchovies with what?"

"On your menu, third down, Kiluvõileib – that's what I had. It's like an open sandwich made with whole anchovies, eggs and homemade rye bread."

"That sounds good, I'll try it."

The waiter appeared and they both ordered the traditional Estonian dish along with lemonade.

"I confess, I do cut the heads off the anchovies," whispered Sarah.

"You won't be alone there," replied Rachel.

Chapter 14

Marjorie awoke to a darkened room. Wondering where she was, she lifted a heavy head from the pillow before realising she was on a cruise with Rachel. Her hand automatically went to her head on remembering she had taken tablets to relieve a migraine. The pain had eased, but had left her feeling groggy.

She reached for the glass of water on the bedside table and reluctantly switched on the overhead light. After blinking a few times, she felt relieved to find the light didn't irritate her head. Mario had instructed her to call him on waking, so she did so.

The eager butler arrived within seconds as if he'd been hovering outside her room.

"Lady Snellthorpe, I worry about you." He smiled sincerely. "Would you like me to open the curtains?"

"Perhaps just a little, please. The room is very dark with them closed, but that's what helped me to sleep."

He walked to the far end of her bedroom and pulled the cord. The heavy full-length drapes opened a couple of feet, allowing light into the room.

"How are you?"

"Much better, thank you. The codeine in those pills made me a little woozy, but it will pass. I'll take the next dose shortly."

"Can I get you anything to eat, ma'am? It's past midday."

"No thank you, just coffee for now. I'm afraid these migraines make me feel sickly. I've got a few biscuits to munch with my pills."

After drinking coffee and taking a second dose of tablets, Marjorie felt well enough to get up. Donning a pair of light sunglasses, she left the room to go for a stroll. Mario had insisted on fussing and she'd had quite enough of his attention.

I expect Rachel put him up to it.

Marjorie looked at her watch: two o'clock. The ship was much quieter than usual, it being a port day, as the majority of passengers and some crew were enjoying the day on land. Others took advantage of the opportunity to stay on board and sit in peace on sun beds, often oversubscribed during sea days.

After breathing in the fresh air, she headed up to the Sky View Lounge where she anticipated it would be relatively quiet. The noise of children screeching as they played in the pool grated, despite being a sound she usually enjoyed. This seemed to be the only hangover from the migraine, reminding her it had not quite gone completely.

The enclosed Sky View was predictably peaceful with just a few dozen people scattered throughout its considerable expanse. She found a settee to park herself on and watched another cruise ship leave the port. People stood on the decks, waving to anyone who would wave back while their ship departed. Marjorie briefly wondered whether their ship was heading to St Petersburg as the *Coral Queen* would be doing later that evening.

A waiter brought her a pot of tea. Another reason Marjorie liked the Sky View Lounge and the atrium café was that they served tea in a pot rather than a mug. There were many things she had learned to tolerate in the modern world, even possessing a mobile phone, but a teabag in a mug was not one of them. Tea has to brew in a teapot and be poured at the right moment into a matching cup and saucer, preferably china rather than the white pottery that had been placed in front of her, but at least it was not a mug.

She smiled at herself.

Marjorie Snellthorpe, you're being a snob.

And on this point, I am happy to be so, replied her alter ego.

Sipping her tea, she heard familiar argumentative voices shattering the peace. Tutting at having her tranquil surroundings invaded, she sat forward to put herself in a position where it would be easier to rise from her seat.

"Lady Snellforpe, you're not leaving, are you?"

Timmy, was it?

Jimmy sat himself on the chair to the side of the settee, blocking her escape route.

"I was just wondering if you'd given any more fought to booking us. The lads are getting snapped up quick wiv bookings." He pulled a diary out of his pocket, reinforcing his point. "Now what date – October, weren't it?"

"Rachel's birthday is in October, but Mr Walker, I'm afraid I cannot commit to a booking until I've met the new lead singer and Rachel has heard him sing."

Not to be put off, Jimmy continued, "Mere formality, Lady Snellforpe – she'll love the new lad wiv the band."

"She may well," Marjorie spoke firmly, "but until she has seen and heard them together, I will not be making a booking."

Noticing the band manager's balloon deflating, Marjorie patted him on the arm.

"Would you like some tea?"

"Nah, don't drink the stuff, mineral water's fine for me."

Please would be nice.

Marjorie caught a waiter's attention and ordered more tea for herself and the water for the disappointed manager.

"Do you have any further information about the unfortunate death of your other lead singer, Mr Walker?"

"Not really. They still don't know whodunit, but I fink they might have arrested his bruvver, Gordon. That's what I 'eard from 'is wife anyway."

"Oh dear. Do you think it was him?"

"I don't fink Gordon could punch 'is way out of a paper bag, Lady Snellforpe, let alone kill 'is bruvver."

That's not what I heard, she thought, but continued, "Why have they arrested him then?"

"Not sure, I fink he got into a fight wiv some young geezer, so Ray says. I fink Dalton's made it worse telling everyone Dom was 'aving an affair wiv Gordon's wife."

"And you don't believe that's likely?"

"Who knows? Dom certainly put it about a bit – tried it on wiv every bird 'e met. Even tried it on wiv my wife."

"Really? How upsetting."

"Yeah, she told 'im where to go then told me straight away. I was angry, I can tell you that for a fact. He's lucky I didn't kill 'im myself. Trouble is, you'd be spoilt for choice wiv the number of people who would have liked to see 'im dead."

"Does that include you, Mr Walker?"

Jimmy scratched his balding head for a moment, rubbed his nose and bit down hard on his chewing gum – a nasty habit Rachel had remarked upon.

"I would 'ave that day, but I was away. By the time I met up wiv Dom, we had a blazing row, 'e promised me 'e would never do it again – even apologised, somefing 'e never did, so I forgave im and we agreed we wouldn't talk about it again. We never did." He sighed wistfully.

"You're lucky your wife didn't fall for his charms, I suppose."

"Yeah, Bee's a smasher to look at – could've 'ad anyone. I don't know what she sees in me, but we really are 'appy, always 'ave been. There's no way I would 'ave let Dom ruin that – no way." He raised his voice.

"Well thankfully, it wasn't ruined. So what makes you think he wasn't having an affair with Gordon's wife?"

"I don't know for sure, but it wasn't 'is style to be shy about it. He would always brag about 'is conquests to the boys. It doesn't fit his MO, if you know what I mean?"

"I see, so you really do believe Dalton is mistaken?"

"Look, Lady Snellforpe, Dalton's a nice lad – but not a lot between the ears. I expect 'e saw Dom wiv some bird and either fought it was Shirley or made the whole thing up. Unless, of course—"

"What?"

"Unless for the first time in 'is life, Dom was keeping 'is big gob shut. Anyway, I'd better go. Shall we meet up tonight after the band's played?"

"Is there another daytime show? I'm not quite the night owl."

"Yeah, tomorrow afternoon on the lido again. We'll meet you after that, then."

"That might not be convenient, Mr Walker, Rachel and I will be ashore for the day. However, we will come to one of the shows as soon as we are able."

Jimmy dropped his head and left Marjorie pondering over what he had told her and trying to remember it all so that she could tell Rachel when she saw her later. The only problem was, her head still felt muzzy from all the tablets she had taken, so she hoped she wouldn't forget everything. Time to return to her room – perhaps she could write it all down once she got there.

Chapter 15

"Did you enjoy your day out, dear?" Marjorie let Rachel into her room. Rachel was pleased to see her friend looking much improved from the morning. The colour had returned to her cheeks and the tension in her brow had almost disappeared.

"It was lovely, thank you, although we missed you. We did the historical tour as planned and visited the Old Town where we had a couple of hours' free time. We also bumped into Shirley Venables—"

"The wife of the angry cruise director." Marjorie finished the sentence for her.

"She happened to be on the same tour bus. We did manage to chat to her, but not for long as Sarah wasn't keen to intrude on her outing."

"Or her own, no doubt – and I can't say I blame her. She doesn't get much time off, does she? Anyway, what did you find out?"

"That she takes a good photo with a mobile phone and that she's a quiet sort of girl. That's about it. She doesn't seem the type to be snogging the likes of Dominic Venables in a public place – I wonder if Dalton's got it wrong. I took a quick peek at the photos on her mobile phone, but there wasn't anything obviously incriminating."

"Maybe Dalton does play economically with the truth as his friends intimated."

"But why lie about something like that? It doesn't make any sense."

"Perhaps he can't help himself. Some people are like that. I knew a girl many years ago who used to invent all sorts of things, so much so that in the end she convinced herself the stories she made up were true. Such keen and elaborate stories she told, could have made it as a successful author, but alas, lies were the undoing of her."

"How so?"

"Not satisfied with telling stories about herself and her own imaginary exploits, she started making up stories about other people – harmless stories at first, but when she got the attention she craved, the stories took on a dark and sinister turn. Any friends she had managed to hang on to soon gave her the cold shoulder."

"Did she tell any stories about you?"

"Oh yes – I had been a scullery maid in a Lord Grayson's household and learned how to pretend to be a lady. After that, I moved to London, pretended to be titled and sucked Ralph in by doing all sorts of creative things! To be honest, I found it amusing, but Ralph flatly refused to allow her in the house afterwards."

"What happened to her?"

"Emigrated, although that might be fiction too. We lost touch. Now, getting back to Dalton, the point is that there isn't always a reason people invent things – perhaps he's insecure. He's certainly not brash like the rest of the people he hangs around with, so it could be his way of drawing attention to himself. Or – he could be telling the truth, of course. Not all women are what they seem, and Shirley Venables may well have been kissing – I can't bring myself to say the other word – on the crew deck. And she could have been the same woman the young man saw in one of the passenger areas."

"Mm, I'll keep an open mind, but I'm more inclined to believe that Dalton made it up or was mistaken about the identity of the woman Dominic Venables was… ah hm… 'kissing'."

"I did discover more information about Mr Dominic Venables." Marjorie rubbed her hands gleefully with a glint in her eye. "Let's have tea before I reveal all. Mario will be arriving shortly with a fresh pot and a selection of pastries. I'm a bit peckish."

If it wasn't absurd, Rachel would have imagined that Marjorie's suite had been bugged as Mario arrived immediately her sentence was finished, carrying a tray laden with food. Rachel stared in disbelief at the pile.

"We'll be having dinner in a couple of hours!"

"I'm sorry, ma'am Rachel, but Lady Snellthorpe has hardly eaten all day, and if you don't mind me saying so, you have room to grow."

Rachel did keep herself in shape with hardly an ounce of fat, so she understood what he meant.

"You can't talk!"

Mario was tall and lean himself with slick black overly creamed hair, and now she looked at him more closely, she wondered if he had actually lost weight since she'd last seen him. After he'd left them, Rachel commented on it to Marjorie.

"Do you suppose he's ill?"

"I can't say I noticed. Remember, I only met him once before and it was under rather traumatic circumstances. Perhaps you should ask Sarah to give him a once-over."

Rachel decided to do just that. Not that Sarah would be able to tell her anything confidential, but she could at least draw her attention to it if he'd not been seen by the medical team recently.

"Okay, back to your Intel. What did you discover?"

Marjorie explained that she'd slept all morning and then got washed and dressed.

"Mario was clucking over me like I was a child," she huffed. Rachel laughed, knowing she had been responsible for that by making him promise to enquire after the old lady while she was out.

"I ended up stretching my legs on deck sixteen and wandered into the Sky View Lounge to sit for a while. I must have been feeling better because it's rather bright in there and I can't abide light during a migraine, but I chose it because it's also quiet and I was worried the noise from children playing might make the headache return." Marjorie went on to describe the goings on of various groups of people who passed through the lounge and watching another cruise ship sail away. "I was about to return to my room when who should turn up at my table but the band manager, Timmy Walker."

"Jimmy."

"That's right, Jimmy – he looks so much more like a Timmy, don't you think? But yes, him – seeing me, he came over to join me, mainly to ask when I might decide to book the band as they get snapped up and such like. I won't bore you with the details. After giving me his sales patter, he finally got on to talking about Dom, as he calls him. For all his car salesmen-type veneer, he did seem genuinely upset about the death."

Rachel thought it was probably more the money he used to make from the singer he was upset about, but didn't want to burst Marjorie's bubble.

"What did he say?"

Marjorie poured another cup of tea and finished off a breaded chicken finger fillet before answering. Rachel saw a glint in her eye as she sipped her tea.

"It seems that this Dominic Venables was a regular Casanova, usually with other people's wives."

"So I gather, but was there any new revelation? Did he say anything about Gordon's wife, Shirley?"

"No, he doesn't hold much truck by anything Dalton says, but he did mention his own wife had a near miss when Mr Venables tried to pull a fast one while Jimmy was out of town. Sounds like she was one of the few who managed to resist the deceased man's charm."

Rachel was thoughtful. She'd imagined Jimmy's wife to be an older woman, but that wouldn't necessarily put the lead singer off, she supposed.

"I know what you're thinking. I thought the same. Turns out his wife has kept herself in shape and is very attractive. He showed me a photograph and she is rather stunning – I told him she looked like an ex model. Jimmy – are you sure it's not Timmy? – laughed and explained he never knew what she saw in him, but they are very much in love."

"So she didn't succumb?"

"Apparently not. She showed Venables the door and informed him she would be telling her husband about his behaviour, and she did."

"That can't have done their working relationship any good."

"That's just it. Jimmy says they had a huge row, Venables assured Jimmy he wouldn't go near his wife again. He says they agreed never to talk of it and carried on as normal."

"How forgiving! Do you believe him?"

"He seemed sincere enough, but he also said that our Mr Venables would make a play for every woman he met."

"That puts me in my place as one of the many then," said Rachel, remembering how he'd made a beeline for her in the bar the night before he'd died.

"You have a far better fish to fry. That other fellow, Ray, said Walker and Venables argued all the time, didn't he?"

"It seems like they all argued, and still do. What a dysfunctional group of people. I'm amazed they didn't come to blows before." Then Rachel remembered that they had done just that a few nights ago.

They finished their tea and decided to get ready for dinner. Rachel returned to her room no nearer to knowing who might be responsible for the death of Dominic Venables, but mentally moving Jimmy higher up the list of suspects. The list that seemed to grow ever longer.

Waverley stood to attention, hovering outside the door to Rachel's suite.

"Mario told me you were with Lady Snellthorpe so I decided to wait," he said gruffly.

Rachel raised her eyebrows quizzically. *You mean you didn't want another ear bashing.* She smiled to herself.

"Will this take long? I'm about to change for dinner. Marjorie and I are meeting an elderly couple we have got to know during the cruise."

Two can play gruff.

"I don't mean to intrude, but I need a statement from you regarding the scuffle yesterday."

"Scuffle? A scuffle is when two people play at it. This seemed more like an unevenly matched boxing contest where one party continues to rain down blows while the other's out cold, but you know that already." She remembered the strength it had taken to pull Gordon off the prone Dave and the fear in the young man's eyes. "I don't want to appear rude, but I really don't have much time." She mellowed. "Perhaps I can come and see you later this evening or tomorrow morning?"

"I'm busy tonight, captain's dinner with some paying guests, but tomorrow morning will be fine. Would nine o'clock suit?"

"That will be fine, see you then."

Waverley turned on his heels and marched along the corridor. Rachel was exasperated, not able to work him out. One minute he was encouraging her to help and the next he was positively standoffish.

Perhaps the captain's told him to keep me out of it again.

Rachel quickly showered and changed into a jade green cocktail dress ready for dinner, choosing white open-toed shoes with a small heel and a deeper toned green stole to cover her shoulders. The mirror revealed a healthy glow developing as a result of spending time in the open air and she opted to apply only a light smattering of makeup without foundation. Then it was time to collect Marjorie, who had arranged for them to meet up with Ron and Mabel for pre-dinner drinks.

Marjorie was ready and waiting, dressed in a black evening dress with matching shoes and a red snug. Her bright-blue eyes twinkled under the light of the corridor.

"You look gorgeous," Rachel told her admiringly.

"And so do you, dear, but then you look divine whatever you wear. It's time young Carlos got his priorities straight."

Rachel's boyfriend, Carlos, had been exceptionally busy with his private detective agency and had been taking jobs that required him travelling both nationally and internationally. A recent case had taken him back to Italy to recover some stolen jewels taken from an estate in Norfolk. Carlos didn't mind travelling to Italy as he still had distant relatives there and it allowed him to catch up with their news. Lady, the Springer Spaniel, had travelled with him on his last trip and helped sniff out the hidden gems.

"If you mean what I think you mean, I'm not ready," said Rachel as she took the old lady's arm and led her down the corridor towards the lifts. Changing the subject, she remarked, "You appear to be a lot better than you did this morning. Has the head cleared?"

"Mostly, just a bit fuzzy, but at my age, fuzziness is not unusual." She laughed. "I'll stay on the wagon tonight, though."

"Good idea," agreed Rachel.

Chapter 16

Sarah hurried into the waiting room towards the end of a hectic surgery and noticed Shirley Venables sitting alone in a corner. She smiled and called her through to the clinic room.

"We meet again."

"Sorry I didn't say anything earlier. I forgot I needed an appointment until my phone beeped a reminder."

"No problem."

Sarah pulled up the woman's medical record on the computer and a reminder flashed as to why she was there, but she asked anyway.

"What can I do for you?"

"My pill implant needs changing."

"Okay. Have you had any problems with it?"

"None, just some spotting which can be annoying at times."

Sarah looked at the screen. Shirley Venables, thirty years old, married with no children. After checking her weight and blood pressure, Sarah asked, "Are you happy to have this implant removed and a replacement in the other arm?"

"Very happy, we're not ready for children." Sarah noticed the other woman's eyes filling up. "I don't want children with my husband."

"I see."

Shirley and Gordon had only recently joined the *Coral Queen* and Sarah hadn't got to know them very well. Obviously the events of the past few days had taken their toll.

"I'm sorry about Gordon being arrested."

"I'm not," said Shirley, starting to cry. Sarah handed her a box of tissues from the desk.

"Would you like to talk about it?" she asked softly. Shirley looked unsure, but Sarah smiled gently, encouraging her to take her time. "Let me get you some water."

After leaving the room to get glasses of water for them both and explaining to Gwen that she might be a while, Sarah returned to find Shirley sitting up straight. She handed over the water and wondered for a minute if the woman would cut and run, but she remained in her chair. Sarah shuffled her own chair round to face Shirley and prodded gently.

"Sometimes it helps to talk."

Shirley looked Sarah in the eye. She had big brown eyes underneath the false eyelashes that glistened with tears.

Beneath the heavy makeup, she would be beautiful.

"Things are not good between us, they haven't been for a long time. I'm grateful for the break."

Sarah was beginning to believe the affair with Dom might have some truth in it. "Go on," she said encouragingly.

"We met on our first cruise contract. He's not good looking, but it didn't matter. We hit if off straight away. He seemed so funny and attentive, he made me feel like a beauty queen.

"After a whirlwind romance, we got married as soon as our contracts finished and we moved to Wales where Gordon originates from. I was happy there for the first six months, but we never went out. He didn't seem to have many friends, but then I realised he just kept me away from them.

"I began to get restless and feel like a prisoner in our home. I complained I was lonely – my family are in Munich. Neither of us could find work locally so we decided to apply to work on cruise ships again as a couple."

"Did you meet his family while you lived in Wales?"

"Only at the wedding. Gordon raged about his parents, he said they preferred his brother who had always been more outgoing. I didn't witness that at the wedding – they seemed a nice couple. They tried to talk to Gordon, but the relationship was strained. Gordon appeared standoffish and waspy whenever they spoke to him. They phoned a few times a week, but Gordon would always end the conversation on a negative note. I started to notice how insecure he could be and blamed his parents, but—"

Her voice cracked and Sarah waited patiently for her to continue. She placed a hand on the other woman's, encouraging her.

"It's not them, it's him. As soon as we started working on the *Jade Queen*, the ship before this one, he became obsessively jealous. Every time I spoke to another man, he would accuse me of having an affair. When I wasn't working, it became easier to be in our room rather than have to explain where I'd been and who I'd seen. I distanced myself from my fellow dancers and they thought I was snubbing them because I thought I was better than them."

Shirley paused again.

"Is he violent?"

"He's never hit me, if that's what you mean, but he's poisonous. He's aggressive without being physical. It started with accusations followed by an apology, but now it's much worse. I'm terrified of him because he shouts all the time – it's exhausting. I've stopped trying to reassure him because he never believes me."

She started to sob.

"But that's not right either. Whatever I do, nothing can convince him that I'm not seeing other men. Chance would be a fine thing – I have to account for my every movement.

"There was a man on the *Jade* – my dance partner, Miquel – he could see I wasn't happy. One day I broke down in training, upset because Gordon had called me a whore. Miquel asked me what was wrong and I told him. He put his arms around me and I cried on his shoulder, but Gordon burst into the room and saw. I became terrified when I saw the hatred in his eyes."

Sarah had seen that look by the crew pool and could understand her fear.

"He pushed Miquel away roughly. Miquel threatened him, but I pleaded with him to go. After that things got worse because he believed he had evidence of my infidelity. I withdrew into a shell and toed the line, hardly daring to speak to anyone – he even kept me away from any female friends. I felt more alone than I had ever been in my life.

"One night, after a blazing row, I told him I couldn't stand it any longer. That if he didn't stop, I would see my senior officer and ask for separation. He seemed shocked and calmed down, and then he applied for this cruise director's job and got it. Now I see he was just plotting to have yet more control. As cruise director, he has a full itinerary of all the activities. Before I could at least get fifteen minutes' peace, but since we've been on board this ship, he's followed me everywhere. He always knows where I am and turns up unannounced. I don't understand how he gets away from his job so often, but he seems to be able to delegate."

Sarah's heart burst with compassion for this woman.

"Was it worse when his brother came on board?"

"Much worse. I only met Dom once before when he sang at our wedding. Gordon warned me he was a womaniser back then. I wondered if it might help Gordon to have family on board, but he was more jealous of him than anyone. I would go so far as to say he hated him."

"Why did he help him to get the job in the first place?" asked Sarah.

"I really don't know – maybe he did kill him."

"Would he be capable of killing his own brother?"

"I've asked myself that question a thousand times and I'm still not sure. I didn't even know he could be physically violent until I heard what he did to that poor passenger on the lido deck. He hated Dom enough to kill him, particularly when he became convinced I was having an affair with him."

"What made him suspect that?" asked Sarah.

"Because it would appear that Dom stole every girlfriend Gordon ever had."

"Did Gordon tell you that?"

"No, Dom did when he made a play for me. He had drunk too much and started bragging about it, told me that since he'd been with every girl his brother had had, a wife would be no different. He grabbed me and kissed me in a public corridor of all places. I was shocked and pushed him away, but not before we had been seen by a young man."

Sarah remembered Dave's story and wondered if this had been the incident.

Shirley's eyes became fiery as she continued. "I told him if he ever touched me again, I would tell Gordon."

"What did he say to that?"

"He laughed in my face and patted me on the head. I hated him for what he'd done to Gordon, and in turn for what he'd done to me. I realised he had caused Gordon's behaviour.

"That night, Gordon accused me of having an affair with his brother. He said someone had told him, and not to deny it. I cried and asked him to go for counselling. I explained we couldn't go on like this, but that riled him even more. For the first time, he terrified me – I really thought he might hit me, but he stormed out and slammed the door. He didn't come back that night. The next day, I heard Dom had been killed and I went numb."

"Did you think Gordon had done it?"

"I wondered, but I can't believe it. I still don't. Yesterday, though, I did speak to my manager, Ms Doherty, about my situation and explained I was finding it difficult to work with Gordon becoming more and more volatile. She said she would try to get me moved, but I feared that would make him worse so I refused. Later, I heard what he'd done to that young man and that he was under house arrest. A few of the girls have been kind to me, so I bunked down on their floor last night. Today when I met you and your friend, it was the first time I've been free in a long time. I realise how unhappy I am and now I just want to get away from him."

Sarah hesitated for a moment. "Stay there, I'll be back in a minute." She asked

Raggie, the medical team steward, to take coffee through to Shirley and explained briefly to Gwen what Shirley had told her. Gwen picked up the telephone.

"Leave it with me. Tell her that by the end of her show tonight, she will have new living quarters."

Sarah told Shirley what Gwen had said. The other woman's eyes lit up.

"Really? Is that possible?"

"Yes, it is. Not only that, but now your husband's under house arrest, he will not be able to follow you around."

Shirley looked at the clock. "I need to get back to work for the second performance. Can we do the implant tomorrow?"

"Yes, of course. Come to morning surgery and I'll do it then."

"Thank you so much." Shirley stood and embraced Sarah then bounced out of the door, emancipated. What an awful situation to find oneself in. Sarah shook her head in disbelief.

"The more time I spend on board this cruise ship, the more I feel like I'm living in some sort of soap opera," said Brigitte, stuffing goulash into her mouth in the officers' restaurant. Brigitte and Bernard had waited for Sarah to finish surgery following her delay. "I told you before, men are scum."

Bernard put his hand on his heart in feigned pain. "I admit some men are, but some women can be unpleasant too, especially ones from France." He sat back in his chair, puffing out his chest in mock victory.

"Stop it, you two, this is serious. That poor woman has been a prisoner in her own marriage."

"You're right. He deserves everything he gets from the sound of it." Bernard was a sensitive man who loved his family dearly and Sarah knew he was just as horrified as she was by the unfolding events. She patted his hand.

"So what happens now?" asked Brigitte.

"As luck would have it, one of the dancers finished her contract this morning and left the ship to stay with her family in Estonia. Gwen spoke with Waverley and Rosa and they have arranged for Shirley to move in with her old roommate, another dancer from the troupe, who is also one of the girls she was out with this morning. Waverley is going to tell the guard outside the room she was sharing with Gordon to bring him to his office for questioning while Shirley goes to pack her things to prevent a scene. He will then be told what has happened. She'll be safe while he remains under house arrest."

"There is one good thing that's come out of this," said Bernard with a smirk on his face.

"That is?" asked Brigitte.

"Murder solved without the need for Rachel." He smiled triumphantly.

"Yes, I suppose he is the most likely candidate, and he certainly had the motive. What a horrible brother, though. No doubt Waverley will be in his element if he can wrap the case up."

"As will the rest of us," said Brigitte. "I really don't like the idea of murderers roaming around the ship."

"Me neither," said Sarah, quietly. "I just hope we're not barking up the wrong tree."

They looked at each other before Bernard raised a glass. "A toast. To no more murders."

"To no more murders." They clinked glasses in celebration.

Chapter 17

Rachel walked Marjorie back to her suite after dinner, insisting the old lady have an early night to allow full recovery from the migraine that had plagued her on and off all day. Marjorie didn't argue, which Rachel took to mean she was still suffering.

"Sleep well, Marjorie. I'll see you in the morning." Rachel kissed her on the cheek.

"Goodnight, Rachel. Enjoy the rest of your evening." Marjorie winked.

After grabbing a summer cardigan from her own suite, Rachel headed off to the Jazz Bar to meet Sarah. Crowds were building up in the entertainment areas as the second run of the theatre show had finished, so Rachel had to negotiate her way through excited cruisers.

She heard the familiar sound of smooth jazz emanating from the bar before she entered. The bar was packed with people enjoying an evening out. Rachel squeezed past a group of elderly men who, on noticing her, parted politely to let her through.

Chivalry isn't dead after all.

Sarah, Brigitte, Bernard and Graham were easy to spot in their officer whites, and Rachel was pleased Gwen was with them as this was more of a rarity. Graham rose from his seat and shook her hand.

"How nice to meet you again, Rachel. I heard you were on board."

"Good to see you too, Dr Bentley, and the rest of you." She smiled. "I take it no emergencies are allowed this evening?"

They laughed, but Rachel spotted the emergency medical bag next to Sarah.

"Alex is dealing with a few minor injuries as we speak and Sarah is on call for us nurses," Gwen explained.

"What can I get you to drink?" asked Graham. "I'm treating the team tonight as a thank you for all their hard work."

"Yes, take advantage, it doesn't happen very often," Bernard teased.

"If you're sure – I'll have a martini and lemonade, please."

Graham made off towards the bar while Bernard and Sarah shuffled along their bench to allow Rachel to join them in their booth. Gwen and Brigitte sat opposite. Rachel looked admiringly around at the medical team, knowing from previous experience that the passengers and crew couldn't be in safer hands if the worst were to happen. They were a happy team who had recovered from the trauma of having a difficult and devious colleague joining them on her previous cruise.

"You're glowing even more than when we met the other night, Rachel," said Bernard. "Blooming, I would say. Love must be suiting you."

Rachel blushed while grinning at the small man who always had a happy demeanour, even under pressure. He had come through a difficult challenge on the previous cruise unscathed, despite finding himself in a vulnerable situation which, in retrospect, could have been extremely dangerous.

"I feel well. Sarah and I had a good day out today, Tallinn is a beautiful city." She chose to ignore his reference to her and Carlos.

"It is indeed. I have been ashore quite a few times there," said Gwen. "Where's Lady Snellthorpe?"

"I sent her to bed – she had a migraine today and couldn't join us on shore, so I wanted her to get some rest. If it was left to her, she would have battled on and joined us here."

"Good for you, that lady needs to take more care of herself." Graham had arrived back with a waiter in tow carrying a tray of drinks. "She's a rare breed these days, a real stalwart."

"I forgot you are acquainted with her." Rachel smiled.

"I knew her husband too, he was just the same. Pride of Britain, people like those two. Take note, Bernard."

"I will, sir." Bernard laughed. "By the way, Rachel, were you told the murder case has been solved without you?" He lowered his voice. "Chief Waverley is certain that the man in the drink was pushed by his brother."

Rachel raised her eyebrows. "Really? Marjorie will be disappointed, she's enjoying playing murder mystery sleuth."

"And you're not?" asked Sarah sceptically.

"Not at all, I'm wounded you should think so. I'm only too pleased if the case is solved. I don't want the reputation of being a bad omen on board this ship. I am well aware how superstitious you sailors are."

"Er, hum, I've never considered myself a sailor," answered Graham.

"Me neither," said Brigitte. "I am a nurse who happens to work on a cruise ship."

"No offence, but you know what I mean." Rachel enjoyed the banter.

"I'm afraid it will take more than a solved case to wipe your reputation clean," Gwen chimed in. "There was still a murder on board, something that only happens when you're cruising."

"Oh dear. In that case, guilty as charged, but hopefully no more. Why has Waverley decided it was Gordon after all? Not that I don't believe it, but there are still plenty of others with a motive."

Brigitte's radio went off, calling her away. "Catch you all tomorrow, I'm meeting up with some friends." She dashed off.

"Goodnight, don't get drunk," shouted Graham.

Sarah lowered her voice and explained what had happened during evening surgery and how Shirley had opened up about her marriage and the longstanding jealousy and control.

"Poor woman," said Rachel. "I actually feel quite sorry for Gordon too, though. Not that it excuses his behaviour towards his wife, but how awful to have a brother like that."

"It takes all sorts," muttered Graham. "I'm not happy this sort of behaviour was going on under our noses. I've checked through the man's medical records and he gets a clean bill of health from the doctors on his previous ship, both mentally and physically. Either he's a good liar, or the assessments weren't thorough enough – the man's clearly unhinged. I'm going to be meeting up with the administrators while we're in Russia and requesting we delve a bit deeper into the mental health of the crew on board our ships. We have to do better."

"Great idea," said Gwen. "Let's not blame ourselves, though. We learn from these incidents and do our best to improve things. However, some will slip through the net, regardless."

"None can be worse than Lauren," said Bernard, bitterly. "She was right under our noses."

"If you lot are going to be doleful, I'm going to bed," said Sarah, which brought the team back into the present. One thing about medics, Rachel had learned, is that they are quick to take advantage of the good times. Before long they were laughing and joking, with Bernard playing the jester that he was.

As the laughter subsided, Graham looked at his watch.

"It's after midnight, I'm going to turn into a frog if I don't get to bed soon." He stood up to leave. "Goodnight, team, we must do this more often."

"Only if he's paying," Bernard joked after the doctor had left.

"Behave yourself, Bernard," scolded Gwen before she turned to Rachel. "Are you coming to the wedding on Sunday?"

"What wedding?" Rachel looked at Sarah, shocked.

"Not me, silly. I haven't given her the invitation yet, Gwen," Sarah replied, leaning down towards her handbag and taking out two envelopes which she handed to Rachel. One was addressed to Lady Snellthorpe and the other was to Rachel herself. Puzzled, she tore open the envelope to find a *Coral Queen* headed wedding invitation:

PLEASE JOIN US FOR THE WEDDING OF

Eva Sipka & Darren Higgs

SUNDAY AT 2PM

THE CORAL CHAPEL

CORAL QUEEN

DINNER AFTERWARDS IN THE CREW CAFÉ FOLLOWED BY DANCING BY THE CREW POOL

"Now I'm even more confused. I know who Eva is, but who's Darren Higgs?"

Sarah lowered her voice. "Jefgeny Popov that was – he changed his name just to be on the safe side."

Rachel beamed. "Oh that's amazing – they're getting married, that's wonderful. How are they? Has Eva had the baby?" Her words tumbled out in her excitement. The couple had been on the previous cruise where Rachel had helped solve a crime.

"Slow down, Rachel. I've been so busy telling you about Jason and me, I forgot to fill you in on all that's happened to them. Eva had the baby last month, a boy named Erik after Jefgeny's – or rather, Darren's friend, who you will remember. Eva is now taking a further six month break to care for the baby and has returned to Slovenia. Darren is still working on board and sending money to support Eva. They

258

have special permission to marry on board this weekend and Captain Jenson will conduct the service. They insisted on waiting until you were taking a cruise before they married because they desperately wanted you to be here for the occasion. As soon as they discovered you were travelling with someone else, they added an invitation for her. They are really looking forward to seeing you."

Rachel grinned from ear to ear. "And I them. I'm so happy. I can't wait to tell Marjorie, she'll be thrilled because I told her all about our adventures last summer."

Rachel bounced back to her stateroom at the end of the evening, but not before putting the invitation under Marjorie's door. She would explain in the morning. What a wonderful evening – no more worries regarding the murder, and a wedding to go to.

Chapter 18

Rachel awoke early. It was dark. She looked at her watch: 5am. Refreshed in spite of having only had a few hours' sleep, she got up and pulled on jogging trousers and sweatshirt, deciding to take advantage of the quiet and go for an early morning run.

A mist hung in the air, hovering over the ship and giving it an eerie feel. The sea looked black beneath the greyness; the sun should have been rising, but Rachel couldn't see it through the grey, despite the ship travelling due east.

After performing some routine stretches by the side rails, she took off at a steady pace along the outside of the deck. Normally she ran on the running track on deck sixteen, but today she wanted a change of scenery so she chose deck fourteen. The deck was silent except for muffled shouting in the distance. She plugged earphones into her ears and switched to music on her phone as she started to jog.

After she'd run twice round the whole deck, the mist began to lift just as she passed the rails overlooking the lido deck.

"What the heck?" She stopped suddenly and stared down at the main pool. "Hey you, stop!"

Rachel raced down the steps to find a man floating face-down in the pool. But before she had the chance to call for help, she felt a blow to the back of her head and everything turned black.

Seeing stars, Rachel found herself struggling for breath, submerged in the pool. Lifting her befuddled and drenched head to the surface, she managed to tread water towards the body and grab the man's jacket, pulling him to the side before clambering out.

An elderly couple were taking a morning stroll on the deck above.

"I need help," Rachel shouted. "Call security and medics."

The couple looked shocked, but did as they were instructed while Rachel tried to haul the wet body out of the water. The elderly man came to her assistance and they managed to pull him out. Dizzy and light-headed, Rachel was relieved to see Brigitte and Graham arriving.

"Help him." Rachel pushed Brigitte away.

More white uniforms were arriving, so Rachel allowed herself to be examined by Alex and put on a stretcher.

"How did he get there?" she heard Waverley shout. "Call Ravanos, now!"

Rachel turned round and recognised the man from the pool was Gordon Venables, coughing and spluttering as he was brought round following resuscitation. Waverley looked down at Rachel, concerned.

"Are you alright?"

After touching the back of her head and feeling the sticky viscosity of blood, Rachel grimaced.

"I'll be fine," she answered, looking at the blood on her hand. "I'm not sure my phone will be, though." Her heart sank as she saw her brand new iPhone floating in the pool. Waverley reached in to pull it out and handed it to her – the screen was blank.

"I want to get her to the infirmary for checks," said Alex. "You guys, take this stretcher." Two pool attendants appeared along with security officers and medics. Then Sarah arrived and took Rachel's hand.

"Come on, let's go."

Pleased to be moving as she was starting to shiver through the wet clothes, Rachel looked up at her friend.

"Is he going to be okay?"

"Yes, thanks to you. We'll talk more when you're out of these soaking clothes. They're bringing him down too. I'm getting flashbacks to your first cruise, Rachel Prince."

"Trying not to think about it," said Rachel. "So much for case solved."

The infirmary buzzed with hurried but controlled activity once they arrived. Rachel felt sleepy and kept being told to stay awake. Sarah helped her out of the sodden clothes and she was glad to be dry, although the white hospital gown was less welcome.

"Great, now I look like something out of *ER*."

The curtains were pulled around her and monitor leads attached to her chest and arm, a clip to her finger. Sarah checked the monitors and wrote notes while Bernard shaved a bit of hair at the nape of Rachel's neck away in order to apply glue to the gash at the back of her head.

"Looks to me like your shoulder took the brunt of whatever hit you, the bruising's already coming out," he said.

The activity outside the curtains sounded distant; Rachel couldn't focus enough to hear what was happening. Then the curtain opened and a worried looking Marjorie appeared.

"My darling girl." The old lady took Rachel's free hand and sat in a chair offered by Sarah. Rachel managed a smile.

"Sorry."

"Don't be. At least you're going to be alright. Don't talk yet. He's hovering outside, itching to come in, but Dr Bentley won't let him just yet."

Rachel knew she meant Waverley and was pleased for now not to see him; she didn't imagine she would make much sense.

Dr Bentley raised his voice. "Look, this is not a circus. Everybody out except the medical team. Sorry, Jack, that includes you. I'll call you when the patients are stable enough to be spoken to, but for now my team need to get on with their jobs without interruption."

Marjorie chuckled which made Rachel smile.

"My spinning head is a bit better now," she said. "Can I have a drink, Sarah, and is the drip necessary?"

"Yes, you can have a drink, and yes, it is necessary. Don't be difficult, you lost a lot of blood."

"Okay, in that case, no problem."

"What would you like to drink, dear?" asked Marjorie. "I'll find that nice medical attendant, Raggie, to get you something."

"Black coffee, please."

"Coming right up." Marjorie left to find Raggie.

"How are you feeling?" asked Sarah.

"Like I've been hit over the head."

"Can you remember what happened?"

"Vaguely. I'm wracking my brains at the minute, but I need to close my eyes."

"Try not to go to sleep, we need to make sure you remain conscious."

"I'll try. Coffee might help. I'm tired from last night, I only had a couple of hours' sleep."

"It did surprise me you were out so early. I was just finishing up treating a passenger when the code blue came through and couldn't have been more astonished to find you lying on a stretcher again. Really, Rachel, what is it about you that attracts violence?" Sarah frowned, her unusually dull hazel brown eyes close to tears.

"I don't know, but I'm here to tell the story. Come on, Sarah, cheer up. It could have been a lot worse."

"That's what bothers me, Rachel. I don't know what I'd do without you. You're my best friend."

Rachel squeezed her hand as Marjorie came back.

"Raggie is bringing coffee for you too, Sarah. You've had a shock," she said kindly.

Sarah smiled at last. "You're right. I'm overreacting again. I'm not rational at the minute."

Rachel sat up and Sarah fluffed up the pillows behind her before checking her monitors and writing notes on her chart at the end of the bed.

Pleased to see her friend appeared to be back in control, Rachel asked, "Can I get rid of these monitors? I feel like a high-tech robot with all these tubes and wires."

Dr Bentley appeared and said good morning tersely while checking the charts, and then he smiled at Rachel.

"It seems you have escaped yet another attack aboard our ship, young lady. You're out of the woods, but someone will need to be with you for the rest of the day, I'm afraid. We can remove the tubes and wires, though."

"Thank you."

"I can be with her," said Marjorie.

"Me too, in between surgeries," said Sarah.

"In that case, you can be discharged. I won't be able to keep Chief Waverley away from you any longer, though. Are you happy to see him before you leave, or would you prefer him to come to your room?"

"Before I leave, but can I have some breakfast first? I'm starving."

"You can indeed, Miss Rachel." Raggie appeared with a pot of coffee. "Trays are on the way from the kitchen. What can I get for you? There's food for everyone."

Jack Waverley was beside himself with worry and could sense his blood pressure rising as the realisation of what had occurred on board his precious ship sank in. He had just started to relax again after concluding that Gordon Venables murdered his brother in a fit of jealous rage. He hadn't been concerned about Gordon's denials – the evidence against him was mounting and Waverley felt sure that once all the facts were gathered, his man would crack. Now, that same man – supposedly under house arrest – had turned up almost dead in the main swimming pool.

After being turfed out of the infirmary, Waverley assigned a security guard to make sure Venables didn't move.

"Where's Ravanos?" he bellowed into his radio as he stormed out of the medical centre.

"He's outside your office, sir," came the reply.

Waverley marched towards his office in a rage, seeing the guard sitting outside.

"Wait there," he snarled.

After unlocking his office and going inside, he called down to the kitchen for coffee and toast, acknowledging the need to calm himself down before interviewing his inept security officer. He kept the blinds closed and put on a relaxation tape before sitting at his desk and practising the deep breathing exercises Graham Bentley had recommended.

The door opened and in came the ever ebullient Brenda with his breakfast. If anyone could help him to relax, it was she.

"I'm so sorry, darling." She placed the tray down and kissed him on the head, then his cheeks, then his lips. He found himself softening in her embrace and kissed her deeply, wishing he didn't have to work.

The lingering kiss came to an end. "You sure know how to make a man feel better."

"I do hope so." She smiled seductively. "Now, eat." She poured him some coffee. "I have to get back to work, but remember, I'm on a promise tonight."

As he watched her leave, he made up his mind – time to remarry. She understood him and was the best thing that had happened to him since his unnecessarily toxic divorce.

He opened the white vertical blinds shielding his office from the corridor and called Ravanos in. The man looked nervous.

"Sit," Waverley commanded.

Ravanos took the seat in front of his desk while he sat behind it and fired up his computer. He looked up at his officer, finding that his anger had dissipated and confusion had replaced it.

"How did Venables end up in the lido swimming pool?"

"I don't know, sir. I thought he was in his room until I got the call."

"Well, Houdini he is not, so admit it, man: did you fall asleep?"

"No, sir, I was awake all night. The only interruption came around 04.30 when one of the crew called me to sort out a disturbance in the corridor. I was only gone a couple of minutes. Just an argument between two of the entertainment team. They calmed down and went to bed."

"Do you think it was a ruse?"

"Looking back, it must have been, sir. Venables must have been ready to slip away; there's no way he would have had time to wake up, get dressed and leave otherwise."

Waverley was thoughtful. "Why would he want to do a disappearing act at that time in the morning? There's nowhere for him to escape to. What was he up to?"

"I'm really sorry, sir."

"Don't worry about it, sounds like we've both been played. I need you to find the crew who distracted you and interview them formally. They will be lucky if I don't get them fired. I'm going back to the medical centre to interview Venables, if Dr Bentley will let me in. At least he's agreed to let me speak to Miss

Prince now that she's well enough to be discharged."

Ravanos heaved a sigh of relief and scurried out of the office before Waverley could change his mind.

Waverley pulled up the security record of Gordon Venables again and scanned through to check he hadn't missed anything. Next of kin, Shirley Venables, wife of twelve months. Enhanced DBS check clear, no name changes, worked for the cruise line for three years, one report of threatening behaviour towards a crewman Miquel Josephs, but complaint dropped by Josephs, and Venables promoted and moved to *Coral Queen* within six weeks.

Why was the charge dropped? There's always a reason – something isn't sitting right.

He picked up the phone.

"Call head office and get me the file on a Miquel Josephs working on the *Jade Queen* – urgently."

Next he pulled up the file on Shirley Venables. Dancer, good at her job, worked for the company for six years then had a break when she married Gordon Venables. Appraisals noted she had not mixed well with the dance troupe, which fitted in with her story. One warning for not turning up to do a show, said she had slept through – not unusual as they all worked long shifts on a cruise ship.

His eyes stopped reading and he studied the incident again, finding it linked to a private doctor's report that he couldn't access. He emailed the chief medical officer on the *Jade Queen* and requested information about the incident, explaining the situation and telling him that he needed to know if Venables was ever violent to his wife. He was beginning to sense he might be getting somewhere.

Still believing Venables to be guilty of murder, he shut down the computer and marched towards the infirmary.

Chapter 19

Marjorie brought some dry clothes from Rachel's room which the younger woman gratefully accepted, and she dressed ready to leave. On opening the curtains, Rachel saw Gordon lying in the bed opposite, looking bemused and terrified. He lifted up his head and stared at Rachel glumly.

"I understand you saved my life, thanks." His lips trembled as he mumbled the words.

"Anyone would have done the same thing," she answered, forcing a smile in spite of the pain in her neck and shoulder. He didn't seem to remember her from either of their previous meetings. "Did you know your attacker?"

"No, he grabbed me from behind and forced me into the pool. The last thing I remember is having my head dunked underwater and struggling to get away with all my might. I panicked because I can't swim, choked as I inhaled water, then everything went black. The next thing I remember is waking up here."

Rachel crossed over to his bedside and looked down on the puny man, remembering how just a couple of days ago he'd been beating the brains out of a young Welshman. Did he realise it was she who had pulled him away? If so, he was giving nothing away.

"I'm Rachel, this is Marjorie."

He looked up, not paying much attention to them, but nodded to Marjorie nonetheless.

"Gordon," he answered quietly. "I'm the cruise director, or should I say, was the cruise director?" His tone turned bitter.

"Was?" questioned Marjorie, obviously ready to continue the subterfuge.

Bernard sat at a desk in the background. Seemingly happy to let the conversation continue, he winked at Rachel.

"They suspect I killed my brother. He went overboard in Copenhagen."

"We are aware of that tragedy," continued Marjorie. "Didn't he fall?"

"They say someone pushed him over. It wouldn't surprise me either way – he drank heavily so could have fallen, and he had enough enemies to warrant murder. But he wasn't pushed by me. Now my wife's left me and I'm under house arrest, plus someone wants to kill me." He looked down at the bed and tears dropped like rain, causing a wet patch to form on the hospital sheet. His bottom lip trembled and his shoulders shook as the emotions were released.

Knowing his wife had taken advantage of the situation to escape from this hideous man didn't bring out too much sympathy from Rachel, but she tried to sound kinder than she felt.

"Do you have any idea who would want to kill you?"

"Not a clue. I don't know that many people on board this ship, apart from the entertainment staff. I guess someone in my brother's band might have it in for me if they think I did him in, but then again, they didn't like him that much either. The only other person who might want to harm me is—"

Waverley entered the infirmary alongside Dr Bentley, interrupting his flow.

"You were saying?" prodded Rachel. Gordon shook his head and looked down at the sheet.

Great timing, Chief.

"Glad to find you looking better, Miss Prince," said Waverley. "May I have a few words?"

"You can use Gwen's office, and then you're free to leave, Miss Prince." Neither the chief of security nor the doctor gave away that they knew Rachel, which she was grateful for. It would help if she managed to speak to Gordon again.

"I'll be back to speak to you soon, Mr Venables," said Waverley tersely.

Gordon nodded acknowledgement before looking down at the sheets again. Rachel and Marjorie followed Waverley to Gwen's office.

"Good to see you looking better, Rachel," said Gwen. "I'll leave you to it. Raggie will bring in a tray of tea and coffee."

"Thank you," said Rachel, grimacing as a pain shot through her neck. "I think I'll sit down, if you don't mind?" She sat down gingerly on the settee in the centre of the office. A large coffee table and two comfortable chairs surrounded it. Gwen's desk was at the rear with a formal office chair behind, similar to the setup in Waverley's office. A Gauguin print decorated the wall and some personal knick-knacks sat on the desk. A few medical journals lay on the large glass coffee table and marble coasters were stacked neatly in a classy looking coaster rack.

Marjorie joined Rachel on the sofa while Waverley placed his muscular frame in one of the chairs. He looked compassionately towards Rachel and warily at Marjorie.

Raggie brought in the tray of drinks and placed them on the table before leaving and closing the door. In spite of his obvious concern, Waverley looked rather chipper, like he had something to celebrate.

Maybe he's cracked the case.

"I can't believe this has happened to you again, Rachel. I can't apologise enough."

Rachel shrugged. "It wasn't your fault."

"Not directly, but the security team let you down nonetheless, and I take full responsibility for that. It appears a diversion occurred – manufactured, we believe – and Gordon Venables slipped out of his room without his guard noticing. The security officer didn't realise he was missing until we called down to find out how he'd escaped."

"I did wonder how he escaped house arrest. What was he up to?"

"We don't know. The team is going through security footage, but the cameras around the lido have been tampered with so I don't hold much hope."

"Do your men not watch the screens like I've seen on television?" asked Marjorie.

"I'm afraid not. Cameras are scattered throughout the ship, but they are not permanently monitored. They record information and we pull them out if an incident occurs. We saved footage of the fight Gordon Venables started the other day, but there's nothing from early this morning on the lido deck."

"I've never noticed those cameras. I did suspect there would be cameras hidden around the ship, though," said Rachel.

"Most of them are around the shops, bars and in the casino. We also scan the periphery of the ship in case anyone goes overboard. The ones on the lido deck aren't that well-hidden, to be honest, so anyone actively looking for them would be able to spot them. We've had more installed since the erm—" he coughed as per his habit "—events of your first cruise when Lady Snellthorpe was attacked. The cruise line is pretty anti surveillance on the whole, but we've had to move with the times – it was only a matter of time. We tread a fine line in relation to security versus privacy, but I can assure you there are no cameras in any private areas."

"I'm pleased about that," said Marjorie. "I do sometimes look at those smoke alarms in the suite and wonder."

"Staterooms, suites and private balconies are completely off limits, I can assure you. We also tend to keep our cameras hidden so as not to alarm passengers. Anyway, I digress. Can I ask what you heard and anything you remember from this morning, Rachel?"

"I didn't hear anything other than Ed Sheeran and Sam Smith."

Waverley looked perplexed.

"Oh, do come on, Chief, get with the times," said Marjorie. "They are two superb young English singer/songwriters and have huge followings."

Waverley coughed again. "I'm a classical fan myself, they must have passed me by."

Marjorie softened. "Me too, actually, but Rachel has introduced me to some of the more recent talents, many of whom I can't tolerate. But even this old girl can listen to the two Rachel mentioned."

"I expect my daughter knows who they are, she's about Rachel's age."

"Hello, you two – I am still here!" Rachel laughed.

"Oh yes, sorry – do continue," said Waverley.

"As I said, I had earphones in, so… hang on a minute, I did hear something just before I put my earphones in. I thought it was a muffled cry, but couldn't be certain so I dismissed it. In retrospect, it could have been Gordon."

"What time was that?"

"I guess it would have been around five-thirty. I'd done about fifteen minutes of stretching and gazing out to sea. After that, I ran a couple of times around deck fourteen, and on my third round the sun broke through the mist and I caught sight of two men in the pool, one being held under. I yelled something and ran down the steps.

"By the time I got to the pool, I saw a man I now know was Gordon Venables face down. The next thing, someone walloped me from behind and I found myself underwater. When I realised what had happened, I was more concerned about Gordon and just about managed to drag him towards the side of the pool and call some passers-by to help."

Waverley took notes. "It was definitely a man?"

"Ninety per cent certain, but I did only get a fleeting glance and they were both in the water. I didn't see him get out of the pool because there's a blind spot when you reach the top of the steps."

"I suppose it's too much to hope that you could give a description?"

"Sorry, it was misty, and the person wore a black hoody and a balaclava like a cat burglar. When I yelled, he turned to look at me, but the sun had disappeared and I only saw a profile. All I can tell you is it looked like a male, six foot tall, average build, wearing black. I didn't even recognise Gordon until I pulled him out of the water."

"I don't understand why he would be out there," said Marjorie. "Surely he wasn't going to swim for it."

Waverley put his notebook in his uniform pocket. "That's what I'm going to find out," he said. "By the way, what were you talking about when I came into the infirmary?"

"He was thanking Rachel for saving his life," said Marjorie.

"Mm." Waverley looked sceptical. "Well if you remember anything else, you know where to find me. I realise I was going to take a statement from you today with regards to the fight you broke up, Rachel, but under the circumstances that won't be necessary. I suspect the cruise line will be contacting you concerning compensation again."

Marjorie, giggling, nudged her. "At this rate, you'll be able to buy your own flat in London."

Waverley trudged off, muttering to himself.

"You are awful to him," Rachel scolded.

"Oh, really? I do quite like the man, and he did seem remarkably happy today, did you notice?"

"Yes, I did think that. I wondered if he had someone in custody for the murder, but obviously not."

"He looks like a man in love to me."

"I hadn't thought of that." Rachel hoped so – she had grown fond of the security chief, in spite of his mood swings. She knew he wanted her on his security team, and once again she pondered whether that might actually be a safer way to cruise.

"At least I'd get my own taser." She uttered her thoughts out loud, much to Marjorie's amusement.

"Come on, young lady. I imagine that blow to the head has addled your brain if you're considering joining cruise ship security."

They walked arm in arm towards the rear of the ship, taking the lift up to their suites.

Chapter 20

Sarah took over from Bernard in the infirmary so that he could help with morning surgery. Gordon had fallen asleep, so she took the opportunity to chat to Jason who was on guard outside to ensure he didn't slip away again. They hadn't been able to meet up for the past few nights due to opposing shifts.

Jason stood as she opened the door and smiled at her affectionately. They knew better than to embrace while on duty, so she settled for the sparkle in his eye.

"I'm glad it's you."

"I volunteered," he answered smugly. "How's our man?"

"Sleeping. What happened? How did he get away?"

"He gave Ravanos the slip, that's all I know. The chief's interviewing your friend, Rachel, to find out if she saw anything. She's brave, that girl, I'll give her that."

Sarah frowned. "Too brave sometimes. I worry about her, but it's in her nature to investigate. I just wish she didn't feel the need to do it on board this ship. It's fine when she's in uniform and armed with radio, whistle, stab vest, truncheon and the like, but here, she's completely unarmed and vulnerable."

He laughed. "The police don't carry whistles anymore, Sarah."

She poked him in the ribs. "You know what I mean."

"The chief still suspects we've got our murderer in there." He nodded towards the infirmary, behind the door.

"Is he right?"

"I guess so. It's not my investigation – he's put me in charge of the stag group and cheerleaders. What a handful they are."

"Lucky you… what do you mean, the cheerleaders?" A stab of jealousy momentarily caused Sarah alarm, but Jason seemed oblivious.

"I'm tasked with making sure the guys in the stag party don't cause them any bother. It's hard when they all seem to be pairing up – I can't tell them not to flirt with each other, much to the chief's disgust."

"How do you find Dave Hughes?"

"Haven't seen a great deal of him. He's quite brawny underneath that weak facade – I did notice him boxing a punch bag in the gym. I don't know how he let Gordon Venables get the better of him – seems like a complete mismatch to me."

"Perhaps he's trying to build up some muscle."

"Maybe, but he's got quite a six pack already."

"Kettle and pot!"

"Yeah, but I spent years in the army having mine drilled into me." He smirked flirtatiously.

Sarah recognised the footsteps coming towards them as Waverley headed their way.

"He looks happy," she whispered.

Jason stood to attention.

"Anything to report?"

"No, sir, he's sleeping. Nurse Bradshaw was just asking about the Welshman, Dave Hughes."

"Hm, I'm sure." Waverley's knowing smile told her their relationship had been rumbled, but then it was his job to be aware of what went on aboard the vessel. "I take it I'm allowed to wake him now?" he asked Sarah.

"Yes, come on through."

Waverley nodded to Jason to follow them and they walked towards the bed where Gordon Venables was out for the count.

Sarah approached him and gently touched his shoulder. "Mr Venables? Gordon?"

He woke, startled momentarily with the appearance of a rabbit in headlights, but calmed when he saw Sarah smiling at him. He looked behind her towards Waverley and Jason and resignation filled his eyes. He sat up slowly.

"Could I have a drink, please?"

"Yes, of course." Sarah handed him a glass of water. "Would you like a hot drink?"

"Tea, please."

"Gentlemen?"

"Tea as well," said Waverley.

"Coffee for me, please." Jason winked at her.

Sarah picked up a phone on the wall and dialled through to Raggie with drinks requests.

"Glad to find you looking better," said Waverley, taking a seat by Gordon's bed and removing a notepad from his pocket. Jason remained standing.

"I suppose you want to know how I got away."

"I know the how, but I don't understand the why."

"I received a phone call from someone saying they needed to meet me urgently about Shirley. They said she was in danger. You wouldn't have listened to me," he said bitterly, "so I called a couple of guys and asked them to distract the security guard from outside my room."

"Very enterprising," answered Waverley caustically.

"Anyway, the guy on the phone told me to meet him on the lido deck by the main pool. He must have been waiting for me in the shadows. As soon as I arrived, he jumped me and pushed me in the pool. I panicked – I can't swim."

Waverley rolled his eyes, disdain evident. "The pool isn't that deep."

"And I'm not that tall," Gordon snapped back. "I was scared; the man had me in the pool before I realised what was happening and he pushed my head underwater. I'm terrified of drowning. I don't remember any more."

"Who was he? Did you see his face?"

"No, it was dull and misty. I heard him say something – it sounded like 'That's for Mam', but it didn't make any sense."

Waverley sighed, frustrated. "Did you recognise the voice? Did he give a name? Anything?"

"I thought I recognised the voice on the phone, but I can't remember where from. He didn't give a name. He wore a balaclava and he was strong, that's all I remember. I didn't get a chance to see anything else. He didn't attack me to converse."

Ignoring the sarcasm, Waverley persevered. "Do you have any idea who it was?"

"No, unless it was one of Dom's mates."

"On that note, are you ready to confess to the murder of your brother?"

Sarah noticed panic fill Gordon's eyes.

They were interrupted by the arrival of drinks and Jason poured them and passed them around, winking at Sarah again.

"I didn't kill my brother. You can't still think I did! Surely, whoever tried to kill me also killed my brother."

"Unless they tried to kill you *because* you killed your brother," retorted Waverley.

Gordon took a deep breath and the panic in his eyes turned to anger – the anger Sarah had witnessed by the crew pool when he'd spoken about his brother.

"You have no evidence I killed him and yet you insist on locking me up. You've no right, and now you've caused my wife to leave me. Where is she?"

"Oh no, Mr Venables, you managed to cause your wife to leave you all by yourself. Fits of jealously, rage, controlling and abusive behaviour. You're a disgrace to our sex." Waverley's face had reddened, a witness to the strain he was under, but he quickly regained control. "Your wife is quite safe now."

"Well I want to see her." Gordon looked desperately to Sarah for help, but she had no inclination to assist in this matter. She shrugged her shoulders.

"That is quite out of the question. Your wife does not wish to be near you. Your employment has been discontinued as of yesterday – the sooner you confess to killing your brother, the sooner I can hand you over to the authorities. We're in Russia presently – I'm sure they will know how to deal with you. Your wife, of course, will remain an employee on board ship."

Gordon's fists clenched. He threw his tea at Waverley, who ducked and the tea hit Jason, soaking his pristine white uniform.

"Really, Chief? Is this necessary?" Sarah snapped as Waverley quickly cuffed Gordon to the bed rail.

"Sorry. Perhaps you'd better go and change," he said to Jason. "I'll take up your post until you get back."

Sarah accompanied Jason outside, handing him a roll of paper towelling used for covering the examination beds, and he thankfully wiped himself down.

"What's got into Waverley?"

Jason laughed. "At least it was only lukewarm tea."

Sarah loved Jason's ability to look on the funny side of life, one of the reasons they got on so well. She also recognised the fierce loyalty to his boss – something he'd learned in the army.

"You have to trust the man next to you has got your back," he'd told her when recounting some of his experiences. Some traumas he wouldn't share and she knew better than to ask – those conversations he reserved for his ex-army friends. Perhaps one day he would tell her.

Sarah returned to the infirmary, finding Waverley and Gordon chatting away like old friends. Bad cop had disappeared for now and good cop was in full flow. As she got closer, she heard them talking about football of all things.

Men! She would never understand them.

While Sarah and Jason were outside the infirmary, Waverley had recognised the funny side of what had happened and, thankful for his own lucky escape, had burst out laughing. Surprisingly, the petulant Gordon had joined in, and before long they were belly laughing at the ridiculousness of the situation.

"I don't mean to hit where it hurts, but you are going to have to come to terms with the fact that your wife wants a break from you," Waverley said as the laughter subsided.

Gordon looked down at his bed sheet. "I've made a right mess of things, haven't I?" Waverley didn't answer, but the look on his face showed concurrence. "How much trouble am I really in?"

"It's not looking good, and now someone wants you dead too."

"I really didn't kill my brother. You've got to believe me. I hated him, yes, and I feared he had got to Shirley. He's always hated me having anything he couldn't take away. Dalton told me they were having an affair. Yes, I could have killed him. I tracked him down that night and told him I'd found out about the affair. He laughed at me and said, 'Not yet'!"

"Did you believe him?"

"I wanted to, and now I do because he would have bragged about it as another conquest. Ironic, isn't it? For once, he'd failed, but I'd already had a go at Shirley."

"So believing your wife was having an affair, you killed him," Waverley persisted.

"No. I felt like it, but I didn't. I decided to tell Rosa he was upsetting passengers –

which was true – and get him the sack. I found out after his death she already planned to sack them all."

"Didn't you get him the job in the first place? Why would you want him fired?"

"I thought it would be fun – we could leave the past behind us. He'd called me, begging me to get him a contract, told me he needed the work, convinced me he'd changed and we could make up, have a fresh start. Stupidly, I agreed. Secretly, I was always his biggest fan, lived in his shadow. Pathetic, isn't it? I just wanted us to be friends, but he had played me like he always did.

"As soon as I saw his smug face coming on board, I realised he hadn't changed one iota. I wanted to punch him in the mouth, but he's always been stronger than me. I'd gone down to greet him, but I turned around and went the other way. He was a bully and a misogynist, but I didn't kill him."

Waverley frowned. Either this man was a brilliant liar, or he was telling the truth, but that would cause huge problems.

Now what?

Gordon continued talking, looking a lot more relaxed. "He was the world's worst brother. He even supported an English football team, for goodness' sake."

"What's wrong with English football teams? I'm a lifelong Chelsea supporter."

"I'm a Cardiff City fan through and through. We didn't do so well in our last match with you guys, though."

Sarah entered the infirmary and raised her eyebrows at Waverley, who smiled back at her.

"No real harm done. It was only tea," he said sheepishly.

Sarah scowled at him, but didn't say anything.

Waverley rose from his chair and unlocked the handcuffs. "I don't think we'll be needing these."

"Thanks." Gordon brightened.

Waverley marched through the doors and took a seat outside, waiting for Jason Goodridge to return.

Chapter 21

Rachel and Marjorie were sitting on the balcony, enjoying watching the activity dockside in the port of St Petersburg, Russia.

"I'm so sorry to have ruined your day out." Rachel apologised for the fourth time.

"You really don't have to be. I've visited the city quite a few times, and at least it's an overnight stopover so perhaps Dr Bentley will clear you for going out tomorrow."

"Oh, no! That's not happening. We're not cancelling the ballet tonight. I know how much you are looking forward to it, and so am I. Sarah and Jason are coming too so we finally get to meet him properly. We're going and that's that."

"I'm not sure, dear. You should rest."

"I've rested since six o'clock this morning. If I have any more rest, I'll go spare." She looked at Marjorie. "If the shoe was on the other foot, you would go."

Marjorie caved. "You're right. I would, but should we ask Dr Bentley?"

"Certainly not, he'll err on the side of caution because he won't want to be liable. We'll just go. We'd better not say anything to Sarah until we get there either or she might dob us in."

"Dob us in? Whatever does that mean?"

"Sorry, I've picked up a few colloquialisms. It means tell on us – snitch and the like."

Marjorie laughed. "Are you ready for some lunch?"

Before Rachel had the chance to answer there was banging at the door. Marjorie let Sarah in.

"Hey, you two. How's the invalid?"

"Feisty," answered Marjorie.

Sarah laughed. "I take it she's being a difficult patient? I'm happy to take over now if you want to go ashore, Marjorie."

"I am here, you know. What is it when someone has been injured? I still have all my faculties despite receiving a blow to the head. Anyway, it's more my shoulder that hurts."

"And your pride by the sounds of it." Sarah joined them on the balcony.

"We were just talking lunch actually," said Marjorie.

"Yes, and I insist we go to the buffet because I'm not sitting still for much longer," said Rachel firmly.

Mario knocked and entered as if on cue. "Lunch, ladies?"

Rachel glared at Sarah. "I suppose this is your doing?"

Sarah shrugged. "Just for today – tomorrow you can be out and about again."

Rachel shot a warning glance to Marjorie, who looked uncomfortable but didn't say anything. They ordered food from the room service menu and hot drinks to go with it.

After Mario left, Rachel looked at Sarah. "Before I forget – have you noticed how thin Mario looks? I'm sure he's losing weight he can't afford to lose."

"I didn't, to be honest – I was focussing on the menu."

"Well take a peek when he returns. There's something not right. He looks gaunt and his eyes look too big for his head. I'm sure they didn't look like that before when we met."

Sarah looked thoughtful. "Does his hair look thinner?"

"I haven't noticed, sorry."

"Okay, but now, back to the patient in hand."

Rachel sighed. "Well at least tell me if they've managed to find out who attacked me this morning."

"No, Waverley interviewed Gordon who said he'd had a call from someone telling him Shirley was in trouble. He admitted to arranging the diversion and went to meet the person who'd allegedly phoned on the lido deck."

"I don't suppose he knows who that was."

"You're right – he doesn't. He said he recognised the voice from somewhere but couldn't place it and that the person said something like 'That's for Mam' when he pushed him under."

"How strange," said Marjorie. "This Gordon doesn't strike me as the most imaginative of men so I assume you and Waverley believe him."

"Yes, we do. I also believe him when he says he didn't kill his brother and I think Waverley has come round to that way of thinking now too."

"So we're back to square one," answered Rachel.

"*We're* not back anywhere. You're not to do any further investigating, Rachel Prince. Let Waverley get on with it."

Marjorie was about to object, but Rachel shook her head in warning. Sarah had gone into protective mode so it was best not to stress her out just yet.

Mario arrived with the lunch, and while he was placing the trays down and serving them, Sarah, true to her word, watched his every move carefully without him being aware.

"Bon appétit, ladies."

Sarah followed him to the door and had a quiet word before returning to the balcony.

"Well?" asked Rachel.

"None of your business," answered her friend.

"That's not fair."

"Okay, I've asked him to come to surgery to see Alex or myself and have some blood tests."

"Is it serious? It's not cancer, is it?" asked Marjorie, looking concerned.

"I don't think so. From my brief observation and his symptoms, it looks like he's got an overactive thyroid, but we'll need to take a history from him and do the blood tests and examine his neck. If it is what I think it is, he should respond well to tablets."

"Why hasn't he sought advice, do you think?" asked Marjorie.

"I don't know. It could be a fear that he'll lose his job if it's something serious."

"Yes, he supports his family in San Salvador, he told me that when I first met him," said Rachel.

Rachel decided not to ask any further questions about Gordon or Mario, and not to give Sarah any clue that she would still be going to the ballet this evening. Marjorie said she would stay on board today to build up her energy for the outing arranged for the next day and Sarah seemed satisfied with that.

They spent the afternoon playing scrabble in the ship's library after Rachel managed to persuade Sarah to allow her out for a little while. Eventually Marjorie was able to reassure Sarah that she would keep an eye on Rachel and that she should go and get ready for her date with Jason. Sarah reluctantly left them to it, but the light in her eyes suggested she would quickly get over any feelings of guilt.

"Thank goodness," Rachel said after she'd left. "I love Sarah to bits, but not when she's playing mother hen."

"You can't blame her for that. She's worried about you, and for that matter, I am too. Are you sure we shouldn't just stay here this evening?"

"Oh please, Marjorie. I'm like a caged tiger. It's fine being on the ship when we're at sea, but I can't bear the thought of not getting on land when I can see it through every window."

"Okay, dear, but I can tell you now: on this occasion, your friend is not going to be happy to see you."

"She will be eventually when she sees I'm alright." Rachel answered more positively than she felt and wondered if she was being foolish. Her head ached, but she wasn't sure if it was psychological, knowing she would be going against medical advice and common sense. But she had committed herself now and wasn't going to back down.

Entry into Russia had been by far the most difficult Rachel had yet encountered during her cruising experiences, but not as onerous as some had suggested it might be. Once they were through Russian security, the tour guide had gathered them together, and while they were on the bus, had advised them to stay in groups and keep their valuables closely guarded.

"Unfortunately, tourists are often targeted by thieves and criminal gangs, but stay together and you will be fine."

The guide was about Rachel's age, her hair dyed ash-blonde and shoulder-length with coppery roots. She had large green eyes and wore dark eyeliner underneath and on the lids, causing them to stand out even more. This was Rachel's first visit to

Russia and she was overly excited at finally being off the ship. From the bus, she observed a vibrant city of people going about their lives. They passed a few landmarks, but Rachel missed the names because of a chattery group in front of her yelling at each other to be heard above the microphone.

"Some people are just plain rude," whispered Marjorie. "They'll be the first to complain if they miss out on directions, mark my words."

Rachel took the old lady's hand. "Never mind, we're going to have a lovely evening. I'm so pleased you agreed to accompany me in my folly. Thank you."

Marjorie raised her eyebrows. "As if I had a choice in the matter."

When they arrived at the theatre, they were surrounded by traders as soon as they got off the bus. Rachel took

Marjorie's arm to protect her, but did manage to buy a Russian Fez.

"Dad's always wanted one of these. I promised I'd get him one."

She bartered the price down with the assistance of the tour guide, who was also keeping a watchful eye on Marjorie to make sure she didn't come to any harm.

They made their way inside the theatre and were led to a four-seater booth where an astonished and miffed Sarah was wide eyed.

Rachel hugged her. "Sorry, but I knew you wouldn't let me come if I'd told you."

"You should know better," Sarah said to Marjorie, who looked suitably admonished.

"Don't blame Marjorie, I insisted. I've been looking forward to this for months, so has Marjorie. Her husband had promised to take her the next time they visited St Petersburg, but he died before he could make good on his promise."

Sarah softened immediately. "I didn't know or we would have brought her with us."

"She wouldn't have wanted to cramp your style." Rachel smiled as she nodded towards Jason, who was entering the booth armed with drinks.

After Sarah got over her initial gobsmacked shock, she excitedly introduced Jason and relaxed just as Rachel had hoped she would. Sarah rarely stayed annoyed for long. Jason was the perfect gentleman, attentive to Sarah, but making sure that Rachel and Marjorie were well looked after. Rachel liked Sarah's new beau and hoped the relationship would flourish. For drinks, she stuck to mineral water at Sarah's insistence, although she wouldn't have wanted to drink alcohol anyway with the sore head she'd neglected to mention.

The Russians appeared to take their ballet very seriously, shushing and tutting at over-enthusiastic tourists who dared to whisper during the performance. The cast performed *Swan Lake*, something Rachel thought should have been familiar because she had heard it mentioned so many times, but she soon realised was not at all so. Watching a ballet in Russia struck her as the most wonderful way to spend an evening and her only regret was that Carlos wasn't there to witness it. He would have looked gorgeous in his tuxedo.

How was she going to tell Carlos she had become embroiled in yet another murder investigation? Come to think of it, why hadn't he phoned today? The IT wizard on board ship had managed to dry her phone out and get it working again and there had been no messages. Her muddled head wouldn't allow her to think for too long, though.

She noticed Marjorie wiping away tears from her eyes and realised that she too was thinking of the man she loved: her late husband. Rachel hoped she had done the right thing by bringing Marjorie and that it wasn't proving too painful. She squeezed the old lady's arm.

During the break, Rachel looked around to see if she recognised anyone from the ship. There had been a couple of tour buses bringing people to the theatre and she hadn't recognised anyone on their bus. It was odd hearing Russian spoken all around her and she wondered how Lucretia Romanov, an opera singer she'd met during the previous cruise, and her oligarch boyfriend Vladimir were. He had been planning to propose on the return journey from New York.

I wonder if they're married.

Her reverie was interrupted by Jason bringing her a fresh glass of mineral water. He was hiding behind a pillar.

"What's the matter?" Sarah asked.

He groaned. "The stags, I just don't want to see them tonight."

"Where are they?" Rachel asked.

"Two o'clock."

The large group of young men, with young women interspersed among them, was sitting on the opposite side of the auditorium.

"I wouldn't have had them down as ballet fans," said Rachel.

"No, but the cheerleaders might be, and bees around the honey pot," said Sarah.

"Or pigs in muck," remarked Marjorie.

Rachel had taken out her binoculars and was observing the group to check they weren't annoying anyone. They seemed remarkably well behaved, considering their history.

"It's alright, they're not up to anything," she reassured Jason. "I can see Dave sporting a large black eye and Tonya hanging on his arm. Exemplary behaviour all round, as far as I can tell. They could have dressed a bit smarter, but other than that you can forget about them."

"They've probably been warned about any run-ins with the Russian police. They wouldn't stand for any nonsense," said Marjorie.

"Looking at him close-up, I think Dave looks familiar, but I don't know why," mumbled Rachel as she put the binoculars down and concentrated on the stage.

The second half was about to begin.

Chapter 22

Rachel slept fitfully as her shoulder continued to cause discomfort, but when morning came, she was in a sound sleep. The ringing of the telephone roused her.

"Hello?"

"Oh Rachel, I'm sorry, I've obviously woken you – would you like to go back to sleep?"

"No, I'm alright. What time is it?"

"Nine o'clock. I waited for as long as I dare, but I know you wanted to join the tour and we need to be dockside by ten."

"I didn't realise it was so late. I'll be with you in twenty minutes. Would you order coffee and croissants to your room?"

"Of course, see you shortly."

Rachel dived out of bed and into the shower, dressed quickly and was ready in fifteen. The only reminder of the previous day's injury appeared to be a bruise to the back of her neck extending over the left shoulder, along with the accompanying pain.

Marjorie was waiting cheerfully and looked pleased when Rachel arrived. "How's the wounded soldier?" she asked, giving Rachel a peck on the cheek.

"Much better, thank you, just a bit of a sore shoulder. I bet you've been awake for hours. Have I missed anything?"

"Not really. Sarah called to check up on you but I dissuaded her from phoning your room, explaining you probably needed a lie in. I promised to let her know if you didn't answer at nine, and she was going to race up here and let herself in. I've called to reassure her that you are quite well."

Rachel headed over to the table and poured herself some coffee while grabbing the croissants and lathering them with butter and jam.

"You know, I don't think I ate much yesterday. I'm starving."

Marjorie gave her *that* frown, telling Rachel without words that she had no idea what it was like to be starving, but refraining from regaling her with a lecture about the starving in Africa as she had on a prior occasion.

Marjorie's suite looked neat and tidy as always with the large flat screen television displaying CNN with the sound muted. The subtitles didn't reveal any good news so Rachel chose not to watch. The old lady had dressed smartly in a warm summer dress with a light cardigan over the top. Although this was a spring cruise, the weather had been exceptionally warm.

"You also missed His Lordship this morning. I wouldn't let him disturb you."

Rachel realised after a moment's confusion she meant Waverley.

"Did he say what he wanted?"

"Him, tell a batty old woman like me? No, he said it wasn't important and that he'd catch you later. I explained we would be out for the whole day. He asked if we could pop to his office after dinner this evening."

"We?" Rachel grinned.

"I'm sure that's what I heard, my hearing isn't so good these days."

"Your hearing is perfect, but I wouldn't go without you anyway."

Marjorie smiled with pleasure at the revelation. She picked up a jacket from the built-in wardrobe and took hold of her handbag.

"It's time we got a move on."

Rachel slurped down the rest of her coffee and, with a mouthful of croissant, ran to her room to clean her teeth and grab a jumper and handbag while Marjorie waited anxiously. By the time they'd picked up Sarah from reception and arrived dockside, their tour crowd had already gathered. The guide ticked them off in more ways than one and they boarded the bus taking them into St Petersburg for a shopping trip and some sightseeing. They were not allowed off ship in Russia except on supervised tours due to visa restrictions.

"Look who's here." Marjorie nudged Rachel and pointed to Ray, Dalton, Nick and another man occupying the long back seat of the bus, too busy talking to notice them.

"That must be the new lead singer," said Rachel.

"Not quite new – remember Nick told us he left previously following a fight with Dominic Venables over a woman. According to Nick, he had more reason to kill Dominic than anyone and had threatened to do so."

"With the best will in the world, we can't place him at the crime scene, more's the pity. I don't want to know, anyway. Let Waverley get on with it."

Rachel thought she recognised the new man but couldn't place him. Marjorie raised her eyebrows and threw Rachel a sceptical look, but didn't go there.

Instead, she said, "Look who else has joined the tour."

Rachel took the aisle seat next to Marjorie while Sarah sat across from them. Shirley Venables climbed on to the bus with the same group of women as she'd been with in Tallinn. She looked happy and attractive.

"And just to complete the party—" It was Rachel's turn to nudge Marjorie, who stood up to find out who she meant. "It's the stag party and the cheerleaders."

"Oh dear, I do hope this doesn't turn out to be a carbon copy of *Murder on the Orient Express*."

"More like *Seven Brides for Seven Brothers* the way they're carrying on. Anyway, there's nowhere to hide a body."

"Behave, you two," Sarah scolded.

The bus passed some of the more popular tourist attractions before stopping at a bazaar where they could use their luncheon vouchers. The tour guide explained they could then spend an hour shopping in the marketplace, but suggested they didn't go off alone and to stick to the Government approved souvenir shops.

"That charge treble the price," remarked Marjorie cynically.

"Don't worry," said Sarah. "We'll wander around the traders' stalls."

After the bus dropped them off, they sauntered into the busy bistro to have lunch. On finding a table, they sat down and perused the menu. Rachel saw Shirley heading towards their table.

"I wanted to thank you for everything you did for me the other day."

Sarah blushed, never comfortable being the centre of attention. "I didn't do anything really, but I'm pleased things are working out for you. It can't be easy."

An embarrassing silence hung in the air until Marjorie broke it.

"Hello, dear. My name is Marjorie – why don't you join us for lunch?"

"Oh, I wouldn't want to impose," said Shirley.

"You wouldn't be imposing, please do join us," Sarah encouraged. "I should have invited you myself. This is Lady Snellthorpe, a friend of mine and Rachel's. Rachel you've already met."

Rachel smiled and pulled out a chair next to her, which Shirley gratefully accepted.

"Thank you and I'm pleased to meet you, Lady Snellthorpe."

Marjorie scowled. "Less of the Lady here, please call me Marjorie."

Rachel studied Shirley while she spoke to Sarah and Marjorie, pleased with how relaxed she seemed. The worry lines that had been so evident on her forehead had disappeared and her demeanour looked generally at ease, with just the occasional frown. Her bright green eyes reflected in the light of the café window.

Marjorie nudged Rachel's foot under the table. "Have you decided what to eat?"

"Sorry, I was miles away." She concentrated on the menu, relieved by the English translation next to the Russian.

"I'll settle for a beef sandwich and tea, I'm not feeling very adventurous today."

The waiter took their lunch vouchers and brought their food. Sarah and Shirley chatted away like old friends.

Marjorie looked pleased with herself. "Now about our shopping. I want to buy Russian stacking dolls – Matryoshka, I believe they are called – for my housekeeper, Mrs Ratton, and for my maid, and a fez for Johnson. Jeremy will be content with a bottle of vodka, and for that matter, so will I. How about you?"

"A Fabergé egg and a tea towel for my mum – she collects tea towels. Matryoshka dolls for my niece, and I'm not sure what to get for Carlos. My brother will settle for vodka I'm sure and his partner will be happy with duty-free perfume."

"We'll find something for Carlos, but I fear if we don't get going, we might run out of time."

They said goodbye to Shirley who rejoined her group to go window shopping.

"Let's hit the stalls, then," said Marjorie, taking charge. "Will you be looking for anything, Sarah?"

"Nothing in particular, but if I spot anything, I'll stop."

After they'd walked around the packed marketplace and made their purchases, time was running out for meeting back at the bus. Marjorie turned out to be a proficient haggler and managed to get everything she needed while helping Rachel with the necessary bartering. Rachel just enjoyed the vibrancy of the market. She took note of the fully armed unsmiling police, who reminded her of how lucky she was not to be armed as a policewoman in the UK. The day would likely come when police had to carry guns – there were already more armed officers than ever before as a result of acts of terrorism, but the temptation to shoot first and ask questions later bothered her a great deal. She often debated it with her colleagues, some of whom were all too eager to carry guns. She hadn't even got to the stage of carrying a taser yet, but would be undertaking training in the near future.

All the security guards on board the *Coral Queen* carried tasers and had access to arms if required, Waverley had told her during one of their many conversations. She wondered how the investigation was progressing.

I expect the killer is one of the people on our bus, she mused uncomfortably. A member of the tribute band would be a likely suspect if suspicion moved away from Gordon.

"Come on, Rachel, you're dawdling." Sarah grabbed her arm. "You need to find something for Carlos. How is he, by the way?"

"I'm not sure. I tried ringing him last night and today, but his phone went straight over to voicemail. The last time I spoke to him, he was in Birmingham, about to break up a dog snatching racket. I'm beginning to worry. I've been so distracted by matters aboard the ship that I hadn't given much thought to it, but now I've tried to contact him without success, it's concerning."

"He's probably in a poor signal area."

"Maybe, but he usually tries to contact me when he knows I'm on land with a signal. We've been two days here and not a word. I'll try his office when we get back to ship."

"Did you hear from him in Tallinn?"

"Just a text saying the Birmingham thing was a bit complicated and not to ring him as he was doing some undercover work in between stakeouts. I thought he was referring to that day, but perhaps he has his phone off if he's still undercover."

"You know what you're both like when you've got something to investigate. I'm sure he'll be in touch today."

Marjorie, aware of Rachel's worry, squeezed her arm. "All will be well. He's sensible and will contact you as soon as he can. Now come on, dear. Let's find him a present. That will cheer you up."

Rachel, trying to extinguish the myriad of scenarios playing out in her head and assuage the feelings of guilt over being too wrapped up in her own problems, followed her friends.

Chapter 23

Shirley Venables entered the room where Sarah had just finished evening surgery. The fearful eyes and pallid face told Sarah something was seriously wrong.

Shirley handed her an envelope.

"What is it?"

The other woman remained mute, but nodded to Sarah to open it. Sarah noticed Shirley trembling as she took out a folded piece of *Coral Queen* headed stationery.

DON'T THINK YOU'VE GOT AWAY WITH IT. THERE'S NO ESCAPE. WATCH YOUR BACK.

The letters had been cobbled together using words from magazines, something like one would see in a television drama.

"I found it under the door of my room when I got back."

Sarah turned over the envelope and saw it was addressed to Shirley using similar cut-out words.

Placing it down on her desk, she said, "We need to show this to security, but I don't want to put any further fingerprints on it." Sarah took a pair of surgical gloves off a shelf and put them on, then slipped the paper back inside the envelope.

She picked up the telephone and called Waverley. There was no reply from his office so she had him radioed to meet them there urgently.

"What does it mean? Got away with what?"

Shirley was too distraught to answer for a few moments.

"I don't know what it means," she said eventually. "The tone is Gordon's, but how could it be? He's in the infirmary, isn't he?"

Sarah took her hand. "No, he was discharged this morning, but he's still under house arrest. Let's go find the security chief and show him the letter."

Sarah quickly explained the situation and where she was going to Gwen.

"I can take the on-call bag with me."

"No you won't. I'll cover until you get back. Brigitte and Bernard are having the evening off."

"Thank you." Sarah was pleased Gwen had come up trumps because she couldn't be sure how long the matter would take. "I'll be back as soon as I can. I'll call you on the radio."

Waverley's office was in darkness when they arrived, so they took a seat outside and waited. Sarah found distracting Shirley difficult and inwardly cursed Waverley for being so slow.

She tried a topic that might help the woman relax. "How did you get into dancing?"

Shirley stopped hand wringing for a moment, but continued to look down at them. Sarah noticed the wedding ring had been removed.

"My mum loved ballet but had to give up due to health problems, so she was determined to encourage me. I took ballet lessons from the age of three, but when I went to my first musical I fell in love with show dancing. I became enthralled by the dancers' creativity that resulted in the show saying so much more than it would have done otherwise. I now know all about choreography, of course, but back then I was mesmerised.

"I turned to my mum at the end of the show and told her that was the kind of dancer I wanted to be. She tried to push me to continue ballet for a while afterwards, but accepted that my heart wasn't in it, so she supported me in taking up dance classes in a local community centre. We didn't have a lot of money, but eventually I got a scholarship to go to a dance school in Berlin. The hardest thing was leaving my mum behind, but she wouldn't have it any other way. She wanted me to fulfil my dreams and I did, until I met Gordon. Now everything's ruined."

"It doesn't need to be," said Sarah gently. "It's tough right now, but it won't be like this forever. You have years of dancing ahead of you and you're really good. Who's saying you won't end up in a West End show some day?"

"Do you think so?"

Wondering if she might have been a little over optimistic, Sarah was relieved to see the looming figure of Waverley heading towards them. He could clearly tell by the look on Shirley's face something was seriously wrong so nodded curtly to Sarah before unlocking his door.

"Come inside, ladies. Please take a seat. Can I get you something to drink?"

"Mineral water for me, please, I'm on call," said Sarah.

"I'll take water too, please. I have a show at nine."

Sarah doubted Shirley would be able to perform, but didn't say anything.

After getting drinks and placing glasses on the coffee table, Waverley sat in a comfy chair opposite the sofa they occupied.

"Would you mind telling me what this is all about?"

Sarah handed him a pair of men's surgical gloves followed by the envelope.

"It's about this."

Waverley dutifully donned the gloves before taking the envelope. Sarah removed hers and stood up to wash the powder off her hands in the small WC at the back of Waverley's office. When she returned, she could see he was studying the contents of the letter.

"I don't understand," he said finally. "Why would someone threaten you? Gordon wouldn't dare."

"Don't you mean he wouldn't be able to?" asked Sarah.

Waverley looked uncomfortable and coughed. "Strictly speaking, he could, but he wouldn't, I'm certain of it."

Both women looked confused, and then Shirley looked angry.

"You let him go! How could you? You told me I would be safe." Her voice rose to screech proportions.

"He gave me his word he would not approach you in any way. Dave Hughes, the man he assaulted, said he didn't want to press charges, said it was a misunderstanding, and I don't have enough evidence to prove Gordon killed his brother. He's no longer under house arrest, but he has to report to my officer, Ravanos, and tell him exactly where he's going whenever he goes out."

Shirley looked terrified and Sarah was incredulous at Waverley's stupidity in letting this potentially dangerous man go. She would speak with Waverley in private about her feelings. She took Shirley's hand to prevent her from saying anything she might regret.

"I assume, then, you will have him re-arrested. The letter can only be from him."

Waverley loosened his collar and placed the letter and envelope carefully in an evidence bag before picking up the telephone.

"Send Ravanos to my office, pronto," he barked.

Poor Ravanos, he was not having an easy time of it. *He might be losing his job at this rate*, thought Sarah.

Ravanos arrived after about five minutes and looked warily at Shirley.

"You wanted to see me, sir?"

"Where's Venables?"

"He's in the crew bar with a few of the entertainment team."

"I need his movements since his release."

Ravanos took a notepad from his pocket. "He was released from house arrest at thirteen hundred. Stayed in his room until fifteen hundred when he reported he was going to the crew dining room for a snack as he hadn't had lunch."

Waverley coughed impatiently at the additional details, but he had asked so he would just have to listen to a blow-by-blow account.

Ravanos continued, "Returned to his room at seventeen hundred, went for dinner in the staff dining room at nineteen-thirty then to the crew bar where he's been ever since."

"Your job now, Ravanos, is to verify those details step by step. I need times and people who can confirm seeing him. Don't leave anything out. I don't suppose he's been in any of the passenger areas?"

"No, sir. You gave strict orders that he was to remain in crew only parts of the ship, sir."

"Quite. Off you go then."

Ravanos got to the door, but Waverley called him back.

"Ravanos, stop. First, I need you to go and find Venables and escort him here. I need to speak to him."

"Yes, sir."

Waverley looked sympathetically towards Shirley. "Mrs Venables, even if your husband did send this letter, it's pure posturing on his part. He wouldn't dare touch you."

"And that's meant to reassure me?" Shirley stared at the chief in disgust.

"Sarah?"

If he hoped for support from Sarah, he wasn't going to get any.

"Come on, Shirley. We will let the chief get on with his job. I expect he will keep a closer eye on your husband from now on," she said caustically. Sarah knew she was sailing close to the wind being subordinate to a senior officer, but she really did wonder if Waverley wasn't getting too long in the tooth for his job. If so, it didn't bode well for finding the killer roaming around the ship.

"I'll do whatever I need to do to keep both passengers and crew safe," he retorted. She felt his eyes boring into the back of her head as she closed the door of his office.

"Don't worry. He might be embarrassed, but he'll do the right thing. He always does," she told Shirley.

"Thank you. Do you mind walking with me to the theatre? I need to get ready for my show, and even though he's not supposed to be in the passenger areas, he'll know exactly where I will be and when. He will have studied my work schedule down to the last detail. I expect he's still been allowed to keep a copy in the room."

Sarah was only too pleased to be of help and walked with Shirley, handing her over to her friends when they arrived at the entertainers' dressing room. She squeezed Shirley's arm and kissed her on the cheek.

"Everything will be fine. You're safe."

After depositing Shirley, Sarah returned to the medical centre to find Gwen in her office.

"Quiet as a mouse for a change," Gwen informed her.

Sarah explained what had gone on and Gwen too looked surprised that Gordon Venables had been allowed to roam free, albeit in the crew areas of the ship.

"Poor Waverley," she said. "I think he's under pressure with the murder investigation and the constant fracas caused by our young stags. He will feel the error of his ways deeply, I fear. Thankfully, no real harm has been done."

"Apart from scaring the poor woman out of her wits," said Sarah. "I don't think Gordon Venables will be allowed out of sight of security again, though."

Chapter 24

Rachel caught sight of Sarah walking hastily away from Waverley's office as she and Marjorie turned a corner to meet with the security chief as arranged. He sat at his desk, staring into space, but when he saw them, he suddenly stood up and walked towards the door. Flustered, he coughed.

"Oh, Rachel, Lady Snellthorpe, do come in."

"You were expecting us?" Rachel had a sneaking suspicion he'd forgotten all about their appointment.

"Yes, of course. Please sit down, can I get you a drink?"

"If you're offering, I'll have a small scotch," said Marjorie.

"Just water for me. I had wine with dinner and I'm meeting Sarah in the Jazz Bar later if she isn't called out."

Waverley handed Marjorie a scotch and pulled a bottle of mineral water from the fridge. Rachel remained impressed with the facilities senior officers had in their offices, but they clearly weren't enough to console the security chief when he had so many conundrums to solve. She wondered if whatever was on his mind had anything to do with Sarah.

"I thought I saw Sarah in the corridor just now."

"Who?"

"Sarah, with Shirley Venables."

Waverley coughed again, indicating to Rachel that it had been her friend's visit that had brought about his ruffled appearance.

"Yes, I'm sure Sarah will tell you about it later anyway as there doesn't seem to be any confidentiality on this ship, so I might as well fill you in. Mrs Venables received a poison-pen letter – well more of a poison-print letter, actually." His attempt at humour couldn't conceal the concern in his voice. "The words were put together from printed matter, probably magazines. Here, take a peek, but don't touch it."

He laid the letter out on the coffee table, contained in a plastic evidence bag. Rachel and Marjorie stared in horror.

"Who would send such a thing?" asked Marjorie. "Don't tell me her husband gave you the slip again." As Marjorie laughed, Rachel noticed the redness rising from Waverley's neck to his face. She shot Marjorie a warning glance to go easy.

"As a matter of fact, I ordered his release this lunchtime on condition he kept us informed of his whereabouts, and I don't know why people all jump to the same conclusion. Why would he send it?" Waverley's defensiveness betrayed his guilt, and even Marjorie gave him a brief look of sympathy.

"You no longer suspect he killed his brother then?" Rachel changed tack.

"No, I don't." Waverley took a drink of water and continued, "Obviously, I can't rule him out completely, which is why I've kept him aboard ship, but it seems unlikely from what he's told me. He's very honest about his rage at his brother, but I think he looked up to him in a way, just couldn't stand up to him. Then that young man said he didn't want to pursue him for assault. He even encouraged me to 'let the poor man go', as he put it – quite benevolent of him, I thought."

"Thankfully not all people are consumed by malice," said Marjorie.

"I may be putting Gordon Venables back under house arrest, though. I can't take the risk of him harming his wife, but if he sent that letter, he's a bigger fool than I gave him credit for. I'll be speaking to him after you ladies have left. I can see he's just arrived."

Waverley walked to the door and spoke to the security guard, Ravanos, as he and Gordon Venables took a seat outside.

"I can see you're busy, so please don't feel the need to delay. Marjorie said you wanted to see me."

"Yes." He glanced towards Marjorie, unsure whether to continue, but decided to do so. "I wanted to ask if you have discovered anything new about the tribute band members. If Venables is innocent, it has to be one of them."

Marjorie gasped and Rachel, flabbergasted, eyed him with suspicion. "Why are you asking me? I thought you wanted us to stay out of your investigation."

Looking flustered, he answered, "I'll explain. One of our security officers, erm, fell down some steps last night and had to be admitted to hospital in St Petersburg." He coughed again and looked at them both, trying to gauge their reaction. Seemingly encouraged, he persevered. "To make matters worse, since early this morning, another guard has gone down with chicken pox, and Dr Bentley says he can't work until all the spots stop blistering. Normally, we would manage, even with two down, but there is so much going on with the stag party, the murder investigation and a spate of robberies. My team is struggling to deal with it all." He rubbed the top of his head where the hairline was visibly receding and sighed. "That's why I took the risk of letting Venables go on condition he remained in the 'crew only' part of the ship, didn't go near his wife and informed Ravanos of his every movement. We can't pick up a replacement for the injured officer until we return to Southampton. Rachel, I can even offer you a temporary contract with excellent remuneration."

His pleading eyes made Rachel laugh. She looked at Marjorie, who was stifling a giggle.

"I don't think so, thank you, but we might do some informal snooping if it doesn't ruin Marjorie's holiday. I haven't spoken to anyone from the band since the gig on the lido deck. They were on our tour bus today but didn't notice us."

"You don't need to worry about me," Marjorie said keenly. "I've been to the ballet in St Petersburg and that was the most important thing for me. Ron and Mabel are sharing the next two trips with us and I'm sure they won't mind looking after this old girl if Rachel needs to be elsewhere. Are you sure you wouldn't like the temporary contract, Rachel? It would give you a trial run to see if you might like to be a security officer in the future."

"How much is a generous remuneration?" Rachel grinned at Waverley.

Waverley relaxed back in his seat and smiled for the first time since they'd entered the office. "It would be more than a month's salary for a few days work. You're also due compensation for the incident yesterday – our insurance negotiator will be in touch about that."

"Thanks again for the offer, but I still don't want to take the contract. I will agree to do some informal investigating. Marjorie and I will see what we can find out, if anything. The murderer obviously believes they've got away with it if Gordon is innocent, but I'm sure you haven't ruled him out entirely?"

"Not at all. I'll take you up on that offer as long as you're both discreet. I can't have you putting yourselves in danger if you're not in our employ. I can't seem to get anything out of that lot anyway. I've done background checks into all three, along with their manager – two of them have been arrested in the past for drugs offences – both cited as personal use. The manager also has a previous conviction for fraud, but over twenty years ago, and nothing since."

"I can guess which two have the drugs offences," said Marjorie.

"Me too, Nick and Ray?"

"For once, Miss Prince, and with respect, Lady Snellthorpe, you're wrong," said Waverley gleefully. "It was the manager Jimmy Walker again, but his crime goes back donkeys' years, and Dalton Delacruz."

"Now that does surprise me, but as you say, it was for personal use and not unheard of in their line of work."

"Did you find out why Ray videoed the fight between Gordon and Dave Hughes?"

"I did enquire, he said it was instinct – apparently gets out his phone whenever he spots an incident – says it might make him rich one day. He surrendered the footage, and to be honest, it was poor quality, jumping all over the place. He was probably drunk when he took the video."

"He won't be giving up the day job, or in his case, the night job, anytime soon, then?" Rachel got up to leave. Marjorie looked at Waverley with a twinkle in her eye.

"You are having a difficult time of it, aren't you?"

"You'd better believe it." He chuckled. "It used to be such a cushy number working on a cruise ship. Things are looking up for me, though." Rachel noticed him fiddling with the box he had shoved in his pocket on their arrival.

Once out of earshot of Waverley's office, Marjorie took Rachel's arm. "Come along, Rachel Prince, this calls for a celebration. We are now semi-official sleuths."

Rachel wasn't convinced about involving Marjorie as she rubbed her left shoulder, still smarting from the pain of her near miss. The last thing she wanted was for Marjorie to be in any danger. She looked at the white-haired old lady fondly and determined she would protect her at all costs.

"What do you suppose he hid in his pocket when we arrived?"

"An engagement ring, of course. He's positively glowing. If that's not a man in love, then I'm in my dotage."

"You're a savvy one, that's for sure, and certainly not in your dotage. I take it you're joining us in the Jazz Bar this evening?"

"If you don't mind? I'm far too excited to sleep. Perhaps we can go to the Culture Lounge or whatever they call it afterwards – might as well get started."

They could feel the beat from the bass throbbing through the floor and drowning out any chance of speaking. Sarah was in uniform and dragging her on-call bag behind her. Marjorie put her fingers in her ears as they squeezed through hordes of middle-aged people enjoying the songs of their youth. Rachel hung on to Marjorie to make sure the frail old lady didn't get pushed over by exuberant patrons.

They managed to snag a recently vacated table in one of the recesses of the nightclub. Rachel caught the eye of a waiter and ordered drinks.

"I'm not sure this is such a good idea. What are we hoping to find out? And I'm decidedly conspicuous in uniform," Sarah complained, not at all happy that Waverley had recruited Rachel and, by implication, Marjorie into his investigation.

Rachel thought her friend could be right: the chances of them discovering anything during a performance were negligible, but Marjorie had seemed so keen, and she didn't want to disappoint her.

"Now we're here, let's just have a drink. We don't have to stay for long."

The three women sat in silence, watching the band perform. The replacement lead singer delivered as loud and competent a rendition as his predecessor, but lacked the charisma of the late Dom Venables. The band played *The Show Must Go On*, which seemed nostalgic and appropriate in view of what had happened.

"We're not going to find out anything. This is silly, and Waverley should not have asked you to get involved at all. I don't know what's got into him." Sarah had continually stated this throughout the evening, and Rachel had done her best to reassure her friend they would be careful. She sighed, knowing that Sarah had a point, especially as she had already been attacked once. Now the killer probably knew who she was. Could one of the band have hit her over the head? It was a disturbing proposition.

Looking at the lead singer, Rachel suddenly realised where she'd seen him before.

"That man, the new lead. He was the guy hanging around the atrium that day Waverley spoke to the rest of the band!" She took out her phone and scrolled past pictures of St Petersburg and Tallinn to the photo of the couple she'd snapped on the day Marjorie had had a migraine. "Look, it's him!"

Sarah and Marjorie studied the photo. "You're right, but what's the significance?" asked Sarah.

"It means they were on board the ship when we arrived in Tallinn. We'd docked and people were leaving the ship, but they didn't have any hand luggage, and Jimmy said the new singer would be joining the cruise that day. I wonder if he's been on board all along, with the woman in the photo. Apparently, he has as much reason as any of them to kill Dom Venables, and now look. He's stepped into his predecessor's shoes very comfortably, don't you think?"

"If you're right, he has to go to the top of the suspect list," said Sarah.

Marjorie looked pleased. "Put us in charge and case solved almost immediately. We do need to check whether he was already on board when we got to Tallinn, though. He might have arrived early and joined the ship that day. It's not impossible."

Marjorie was right. They needed to find out the man's identity and when he joined the vessel, but they seemed to be getting somewhere at last.

"On that note, shall we call it a night?" Rachel asked. The others agreed, and as if on cue, Sarah's radio beeped, calling her to a medical incident.

Chapter 25

The *Coral Queen* docked in Helsinki, Finland on Sunday morning, where Rachel and Marjorie took a private tour to the Nuuksio Reindeer Park. Marjorie had expressed an interest in visiting the park when they were making plans the day before, but time was limited due to the need to be back for the wedding of Eva and Darren (formerly Jefgeny). Ron and Mabel chipped in with the hiring of a private car, giving them the opportunity to do both.

Rachel would have liked to have seen more of Helsinki, but didn't want to miss the wedding, and as Sarah had been asked to work, she had decided to shelve the ice bar experience for a future cruise. Marjorie narrowed the options down to either seeing reindeers close up or heading to town for shopping. Rachel thought this was a no brainer.

"I'll take the reindeers."

The delight on Marjorie's face confirmed she had made the right choice. They were duly rewarded with a pleasant and comfortable car journey, plus the enchanting experience of being able to feed the reindeers by hand.

"Such gentle and placid creatures," remarked Marjorie.

Rachel agreed: they oozed calm, and for an hour, any concern over the investigation into her own attack and the murder of Dominic Venables was dissipated by the serenity of the magical experience among the beautiful reindeers.

"It's like all my childhood dreams come true. The idea of walking among the reindeers and meeting Rudolph was always far more exciting to me than receiving presents."

"What an extraordinary child you must have been," said Marjorie wistfully.

"Don't get me wrong, I still liked the presents," Rachel added, "but I love animals. Sarah would have enjoyed this, I'm sure. If she hadn't been a nurse, she would have been a vet."

"Where is she?" asked Mabel.

"She's on duty, doing morning surgery, and then she's helping decorate the crew area ready for the wedding later."

One of the reindeers interrupted the conversation, giving Rachel a gentle nudge, requesting more food. She giggled.

"Alright, you, here, take some." The plucky animal took the food from Rachel's hand.

After taking photos, feeding the animals and wandering around the park for an hour, they retired to a tepee where a log fire burned brightly in a central fire pit.

Marjorie had been as excitable as Rachel all morning and was now in her element.

"How delightful," she said. "I love the smell of forest and burning wood."

"Well I'm loving the aroma of that coffee," said Mabel. "Let's find a seat."

They sat on fur-covered benches close to the log fire. The older people had chilled off, having spent so much time outside – it was a clear day, but with a brisk wind blowing, the temperature had dipped into the late teens. They soon warmed up when served traditional coffee and freshly made cinnamon cake.

The outing ended too soon for Rachel, who would have loved to have gone for a long walk through the national park. She determined to come back one day and do just that. The private car driver returned them safely to the ship and received a generous tip from Ron for his trouble.

On exiting the taxi, they heard the loud voices of Nick, Ray and the new lead singer, providing Rachel with a stark reminder of her promise to Waverley the day before. She groaned, attracting inquisitive looks from Ron and Mabel who knew all about the death of the obnoxious singer, but not about the attack on Rachel, or her and Marjorie's part in the investigation.

"Is something the matter?" asked Mabel.

"I enjoyed being out in the countryside for a while, that's all. Now I have to decide what to wear to a wedding!"

"What exciting lives you two lead. We need to get out more, Mabel." Ron put his arm affectionately around his wife's shoulder.

The company parted ways as Ron and Mabel were taking a shuttle bus into the city centre. Marjorie paused to purchase some souvenirs before going through port security.

Rachel watched the rowdy group of musicians who appeared to be leaving to go out for the afternoon. Dalton and Jimmy weren't with them, but a woman appeared from one of the souvenir shops and joined them. It was the woman Rachel had seen with the replacement lead singer a few days before, for certain.

I must remember to ask Waverley who they are and when they first boarded the ship. If they were on board prior to the murder, it added to the likelihood that one or both of them could have been involved in Dom's death.

Did the other members of the band realise they were on board?

Another disturbing thought entered Rachel's head: the whole band might be implicated, making Marjorie's flippant remark about *Murder on the Orient Express* a chilling possibility.

Surely not?

The entourage passed within inches of Rachel, but were too wrapped up in conversation to notice her. It was the first time she had seen them laughing and joking with no arguments. Rachel's gaze followed them until they boarded the next shuttle bus heading into town.

It took ages to decide what to wear to the wedding, the dilemma being that Rachel had only brought a mixture of casual clothes and evening dresses, but nothing in-between. Finally, she settled on an aquamarine cocktail dress, white stiletto shoes, a white jacket and handbag to match.

Having spent so much time choosing a dress, she had little time to do anything with her hair, so the long blonde mane was quickly brushed through and tonged into loosely flowing waves. Marjorie was already walking along the back corridor towards her room as Rachel dashed out.

"I see you didn't have any problem choosing what to wear, elegant as always." Rachel loved Marjorie's outfit: a lush pink suit with matching fascinator. It was the perfect choice for a wedding.

"Coming from someone who would look beautiful in a bin bag, that's rich."

Rachel took her friend's arm and they made their way upstairs to the chapel, arriving suitably early. Rachel spotted Jefgeny, now Darren, standing nervously at the front, talking to friends. The chapel was already two-thirds full with crew from all over the ship. Sarah called them over to where the medical team was seated in a row.

"We saved you seats."

The medical officers stood out from the other guests because of their whites and gold striped epaulettes. Rachel greeted them with a cheery hello as Marjorie sat next to Sarah and Rachel sat next to her.

"I do hope nobody gets ill." Marjorie leaned over to address Dr Graham Bentley, whom she and her husband had known for years. "Otherwise, young Graham, you will have to leave discreetly."

Rachel never asked why Marjorie called the senior medical officer, who had to be in his fifties, 'young Graham'. It was obviously a private joke shared between them.

"Don't you worry, Lady Snellthorpe, our French angel can deal with most things."

Brigitte was the only absentee from the medical team. She had been at home in

France when the rest of them had got to know Eva and Jefgeny.

Rachel recognised a few of the crew from the casino where Eva worked and could hear a group of men speaking Russian.

"I assume they're from engineering?" she questioned.

"Yes, the groom's friends. The best man is one of them. It's such a shame his sister can't be here, but it would be too dangerous for him," Sarah answered.

Jefgeny had been required to sever all ties with family when he bravely reported a conspiracy at a company he worked for in a prior life, hence his new name.

"I can't get used to thinking of him as Darren. Is Eva's family here?"

"Her mother's over there." Sarah pointed to a lady in her fifties with tightly pursed thin lips, wearing a floral dress.

She looked austere, in spite of the brightly coloured attire.

"She doesn't look very happy considering it's her daughter's wedding," Rachel whispered.

"Rumour has it she doesn't approve of her daughter marrying a Russian. That's Eva's sister and brother-in-law next to her. Apparently the mother doesn't approve of the brother-in-law either, so at least Darren will be in good company."

"Is that little Erik?" Rachel saw a baby wrapped in a lime-green shawl being held by Eva's sister.

"Yes, he's gorgeous. I've already had a cuddle."

Jefgeny/Darren spotted Rachel and made a beeline for her. Before she could stand up, he'd smothered her in a warm embrace.

"We were so pleased you accepted our invitation. I can't thank you enough for everything you did. You, Sarah and Dr Romano."

Alex Romano and Sarah still worked closely with the Russian engineer to deal with his alcohol addiction and the beginnings of liver cirrhosis. Rachel was thrilled to see him looking so happy. There was still a slight discolouration to his skin, but his emerald eyes shone brightly now that he was overcoming his problems.

"It's wonderful to see you too, I was delighted to be invited. This is my friend, Marjorie."

Darren bowed the top half of his body to Marjorie. "I am honoured you are attending our wedding, Lady Snellthorpe."

Ship's etiquette even applied to weddings, it seemed.

Darren seemed uncomfortable momentarily. Marjorie sensed his unease and dispensed with any class barriers immediately.

"Do call me Marjorie. All my friends do, and any friend of Rachel's is a friend of mine." She took his hand. "Is that your son over there?"

The Russian's chest almost burst out of his ill-fitting suit as he proudly collected the baby and brought him over to them.

"This is Erik Higgs, we gave him my new surname."

Marjorie cooed over the baby and soon found herself holding the young Erik as the groom was retrieved by the best man. Captain Jensen arrived along with Waverley and they shook hands with Darren before checking on last-minute details with the pianist.

The chapel went silent as Eva arrived, wearing a traditional white wedding dress and veil. The dress was simple in design with a round neck and the minimum of fuss. Eva was walked down the chapel aisle by a man in his fifties.

"Her father," Sarah mouthed.

"Thank heavens he looks happier than her mother," Marjorie whispered.

The ceremony was simple and traditional, verging on Catholic as both bride and groom came from Catholic backgrounds. Captain Jensen officiated with an ease that demonstrated his experience. As soon as the ceremony was over, he congratulated the couple and departed at a polite juncture, understanding that his presence would suffocate the crew's joy and prevent them from being themselves.

Marjorie had held Erik throughout the service and he'd drifted off to sleep in the comfort of her arms.

"He reminds me of Jeremy when he was a boy. I do miss not having grandchildren, but Jeremy's never shown any interest in having children and his second wife is a socialite. I can't ever imagine her having children, even though she's twenty years younger than my son."

Rachel squeezed her arm.

The wedding attendees gathered round in groups and began to vacate the chapel after being advised food and soft drinks would be served in the crew café and alcohol in the bar. Rachel and Marjorie decided to leave after the service as they didn't want to intrude or make anyone uneasy. Darren and Eva came to collect Erik, and Darren hugged Rachel again while Eva thanked them for attending.

"It was a lovely service," said Rachel.

"Thank you. I am the happiest man in the world," Darren announced.

As the new Mr and Mrs Higgs left, Rachel thought he certainly looked it.

Chapter 26

Rachel and Marjorie opted for a table on deck fourteen overlooking the lido deck where a live band was playing in honour of the sailaway party.

"Time's rapidly passing and we are no nearer to finding out whodunit!" said Marjorie petulantly.

"Waverley told me after the wedding he's now going back to the theory of it being an accident. He's even considering allowing Gordon Venables loose again and back to work!"

"That would be a mistake, I fear, if only for the sake of his downtrodden wife. It's traumatic enough for a woman to try and escape the clutches of a dangerous and controlling man without being confined on board a cruise ship with him."

"In Waverley's defence, he did emphasise that Gordon would be sacked if he made any attempt to contact his wife during the sailing. He must be under pressure from above with Gordon's deputy having to stand in for him and others covering her work. If he is allowed back, Gordon will be transferred to another ship as soon as possible."

"Be it on their head if the cruise line is happy to employ a man who presents a real danger to his wife and violently attacks a passenger."

"Ah, there is also news on that front. Waverley found out quite by chance during his routine background checks that Dominic Venables had a son. Guess what the son's name is?"

"Is it Dave Hughes, by any chance?"

"You guessed it! His mother never married, but his father on the birth certificate is registered as Dominic

Venables. The information only came to light after Waverley pulled up a historic assault charge citing Venables as the victim. The attacker, a teenager, went for him during a gig in Cardiff. The teenager was named as Dave Hughes, but he got off with a caution after police put it down to a 'domestic'. Apparently, the boy's mother explained her son was angry about being abandoned as a baby and Venables didn't press charges. Waverley interviewed Hughes again today and it turns out he and his estranged father had been communicating via Facebook, and when he heard his dad's band would be playing on board the *Coral Queen*, Dave persuaded his best friend to hold his stag do on board – sort of a final effort. It seems he imagined a great reconciliation."

"Well, that adds a new flavour to the pot, doesn't it? It seems our list of suspects is increasing."

Rachel acknowledged the fact. "Waverley thinks Hughes caused that fight deliberately because of the friction between his father and Gordon, who has no idea that the young man is his nephew."

"I suppose that's possible, but it seems a bit extreme. How would he know how his uncle would react?"

"I wonder if his estranged father had told him about Gordon's weak spot. Dom probably bragged about how he would get Shirley Venables to sleep with him – he was certainly arrogant enough to say something like that."

"It might have been better for Dave Hughes not to have become acquainted with his father, if that's the case. If he did provoke the fight, it explains why he dropped the charges and encouraged the chief to release Gordon Venables.

Perhaps, unlike his father, he has a conscience."

"We only have his word he patched things up with his father, though," said Rachel as she stared into her empty glass.

"You're right. He does need adding to the suspect list. Did you find anything on the replacement lead singer?"

"No, Waverley hasn't looked into him, but promised he'll check and come back to me."

"We really are no closer to the truth. Do you imagine it could have been an accident?"

"Not in a million years. I suspect someone wanted it to look like that, and if Gordon is innocent, the murderer framed him deliberately on realising murder was suspected."

"Or found it convenient."

"Yes. We still can't rule Gordon out, but he goes to the bottom of the list for now. Trouble is with so many candidates, I'm no longer sure who should be at the top. We will keep our new lead singer up there as a question mark until we find out when he boarded."

"Agreed. I would also put Nick Garrett up there. He's a nasty piece of work and there was obviously a lot of friction between him and his so-called friend."

Rachel wrote the two names down along with possible motives. "I think we need to put Dave Hughes up top now too. Family feuds run deep, and if he has an abandonment grudge, he may well have argued with his father. He had obviously been violent towards him previously."

"Then there's Timmy Walker."

"Jimmy," Rachel corrected automatically.

"Yes, Jimmy Walker – I still think he looks like a Timmy – a man who had a lot to lose if the band walked away from him.

We also only have his word that he forgave Venables for trying to seduce his wife."

Rachel added the two names. "That leaves Ray Lynch and Dalton Delacruz."

"There doesn't seem to be much of a motive for either of them to kill the man. Lynch seems happy enough with his role as the drummer and all we have on Dalton is that he is economical with the truth."

"Unless his leaning towards fantasies extended to arguing with Venables, who found out Dalton had told his brother about his attempted seduction of Shirley. That doesn't make sense, though, because Dom didn't seem to mind who found out. In fact, he would probably have revelled in it. Those two join Gordon at the bottom of the list for now."

"And there is one more," Marjorie said thoughtfully.

"Who?"

"Shirley Venables. She had every reason to want Dominic Venables dead – already suffering a life of torment with an over-controlling husband, frightened at what her husband might do if he became convinced she was having an affair with his brother, and knowing that either way, her husband wouldn't believe her."

"I must admit, I hadn't put Shirley in the frame, but I suppose she and Dom might have argued, and the argument could have gotten out of hand. Knowing what we do of the Venables ego, we can assume he wouldn't have backed down, and a woman desperate for respite from the false accusations of her husband may understandably have turned to violence, however unlikely. Perhaps he attacked her and she defended herself. The only problem with that is I'm sure it was a man in the pool trying to kill Gordon."

"Do you know that for certain?"

"Almost, but I didn't get a clear look at him because of the mist, and until I shouted, he had his back to me. But the shape looked like that of a man, and I'm pretty sure my recollection doesn't fit Shirley's frame. Gordon also said it was a man."

"What if he's lying? If he did suspect his wife, it would explain the accusation in that letter she received, wouldn't it?"

Rachel mulled it over for a moment and accepted the possibility. "We'll add her to the bottom of the list, but I just don't have Shirley Venables down as a cold-blooded killer."

"No," said Marjorie. "But as you suggested, if the first incident turns out not to have been an accident, even if it was self-defence, and she had reason to believe her husband suspected her, he would have had permanent leverage over her. She's desperate enough to be free of him."

"The hole in this theory is that a man called Gordon on the telephone to say his wife could be in danger. Shirley wouldn't be strong enough to push him in the water, and by all accounts, he was already under suspicion for the murder and locked up. I can't see her putting herself at risk in that way." Rachel caught the eye of a waiter. "I need a martini – our list has just grown!"

After dinner, Rachel walked Marjorie back to her suite. It had been a busy day and she wanted her friend to get some rest. On arrival back in her own suite, she decided to email Carlos again. There had been no reply from his office phone or his mobile the day before, and worry had been building up in her throughout today when she didn't hear from him again.

After emailing, she opened the doors on to the balcony and found herself imagining different scenarios about where Carlos was, none of them pleasant. When he didn't contact her after they'd docked in Russia, initially she'd felt relieved, not wanting to tell him about the attack, but now concern had set in. It was nearly four days since receiving the last text, and the tension was now setting her nerves on edge. Marjorie had been doing her best to keep her mind occupied, and discussing the list of suspects had helped.

She pulled the suspect list out of her handbag and placed it on the table. The only sounds she could hear came from the breaking of the Baltic waves against the side of the ship to her left. The scene was eerily black.

During their briefing – Marjorie had taken to calling the meetings 'briefings' or 'war councils' – they'd decided to follow the stag party on their tour the following day. A quick call to Waverley and a bit of checking on his part had revealed the boys were booked on a Stockholm sightseeing excursion, and Sarah had reluctantly agreed to join Rachel and Marjorie for the same excursion. The excursions desk was closed, but Waverley had called one of the team in to provide tickets for three.

When Waverley called her suite to confirm that the excursion was booked, Rachel went through the suspect list briefly over the telephone and he agreed they should continue to investigate, but was still hoping to close the case as an accident/unexplained death. He reasoned the attack on her and Gordon could have come from one of the band, convinced Gordon had murdered their friend. The coroner in Copenhagen didn't have enough evidence to conclude that it was murder, particularly as she had since discovered evidence of high levels of drugs and alcohol in the victim's system. As the drug found in his system turned out to be LSD, the coroner explained an alternative scenario to Waverley, suggesting the man may have thought he could fly, apparently a common hallucination linked to LSD use. Waverley appeared to be coming to the same conclusion.

Much to Rachel's disgust, Gordon Venables had been reinstated as cruise director on condition he stayed away from his wife.

"I told him, if he's seen within one hundred yards of her, he will be in the brig," Waverley assured Rachel.

Dr Bentley was none too happy about the situation either, Sarah told her when she phoned after surgery.

"He's worried. He says an obsessive man like that is unlikely to leave her alone. I'm frightened for her, Rachel."

Rachel had to agree. Waverley was taking a huge risk with this one and she couldn't work out why. From what she had known of him in their previous dealings, he made mistakes, but he didn't strike her as a risk taker. What he was doing now seemed out of character.

He can't have told the cruise line about the attack on the passenger.

Rachel found herself equally surprised Captain Jensen had agreed to the man's reinstatement. This reckless behaviour didn't make sense, unless there was something Waverley wasn't telling her.

The sound of her mobile telephone ringing made her jump from her reverie. Leaping up from the table, she almost slipped, realising she hadn't even kicked off her stilettos from the wedding.

Where was her phone? She clambered over the chair that had fallen to the floor and, dashing into the sitting room of her suite, saw the phone on the sofa. She looked at the screen and pressed the answer button.

"Carlos, where have you been? I've been so worried about you."

"Sorry, it's not Carlos."

"Is that you, Greg?" asked Rachel, recognising the voice of Carlos's assistant.

"Yes, he asked me to call you yesterday, but I was following a bloke around all day and I forgot."

"So where is he and why have you got his phone?"

"I don't have all the facts because he's gone off grid on this one. It turns out the case he's working on is much bigger than one missing dog. He said there could be a trace on his phone so he gave it to me to put them off the scent, asking me to let you know. He picked up a pay-as-you-go and was heading up to the Scottish Highlands. That was on Friday. He texted my number on Saturday to tell me he was following up another lead and had boarded a ferry to Dublin."

"I see," said Rachel, trying to control the palpitations pounding through her chest. She didn't know whether to laugh or cry. "Is he in any danger?"

"Nothing he can't handle, Rachel. Don't worry, he can take care of himself."

"Is Lady with him?"

"Yeah, it's thanks to her that he's got this far, he says. She sniffed out a secret room when he went to collect the missing dog. Turned out they found cages full of designer puppies, stolen to order. He was livid – him and his detective friend cajoled the guy into helping them with their enquiries on condition he gets some leniency."

"Okay, thanks for telling me. Oh, and Greg?"

"What?"

"Next time he asks you to contact me, make sure you do it the same day."

He sounded suitably rebuked. "Sorry, promise," he said, ending the call.

Rachel felt most of the tension dissipating. As she sighed deeply and looked heavenwards, she prayed, "Thank you, Lord. Why on earth didn't I just trust you in the first place?"

Her father had always told her it was much harder to have faith when trials came and things didn't go to plan, and she had to admit that on this occasion, her father was right.

Chapter 27

It had been a frustrating day. Rachel had found it difficult to concentrate on the beautiful city of Stockholm because she had been champing at the bit to find out why Dave Hughes wasn't with his friends on the tour and still fretting over the whereabouts of Carlos. Marjorie and Sarah made the best of the trip, annoyingly determined to look on the bright side of everything while Rachel took a rare journey into the doldrums. The other two women allowed her space, sensing her mood, but even that made her miserable.

When they got back to the ship, Sarah put her arm around her friend.

"Oh Sarah, Marjorie, I'm sorry. I've been a right pain in the butt today; I don't understand what came over me."

"Well you did get a blow to the head." Sarah laughed, clearly detecting it was alright to joke again.

"You do have a lot on your mind," said Marjorie kindly.

"That's no excuse. Only last night, I was relieved to find out Carlos was safe and thanking God, and today I behave like a petulant schoolgirl."

"It's the adrenaline drop," explained Sarah. "You've been on tenterhooks for days with adrenaline and cortisone coursing through the veins, and those hormones have plummeted today, leaving you feeling drained. From one adrenaline junkie to another, trust me, it's quite normal."

Rachel slapped her head. "You're right – you know what else? I haven't been running or gone to the gym since Friday – no wonder I'm so grouchy." The realisation that there was a cause for her mood immediately made her feel better. "How strange, I'm fine now."

Sarah mock wiped her brow. "Thank goodness for that."

As they passed through security, they saw Waverley hanging around in the background. He nodded curtly, indicating not to speak, so they passed on by.

"I wonder what he's up to," said Marjorie when they alighted the lift on deck four and headed to Creams Patisserie, one of their favourite haunts.

"Not sure," said Rachel. "It wouldn't surprise me if it's to do with Gordon Venables. I was thinking about the whole situation with him last night and something doesn't sit right."

"I thought the same," said Sarah. "Either Waverley's lost his marbles or he's up to something."

"Oh, you mean he might be using him as a kind of bait," said Marjorie.

"Something like that, because even if Dom Venables did imagine he was a bird and try to fly off the balcony, the attack on Gordon was very real. I can assure you of that from the residual pain in my shoulder. There's still the evidence that Dom was unconscious on hitting the water, which they all seem to be conveniently forgetting."

"I think you're right," said Marjorie. "Of course, he's putting Gordon out there to see if there's another attack on his life. But Waverley told us he was short-staffed – surely he doesn't have spare security guards who can follow him?"

"They have caught the thief stealing jewellery from passenger rooms, which has helped," Sarah explained. "Sadly it was a cabin steward whose contract hadn't been renewed. We all hate it when any of the crew commits crimes like that – it looks bad on us all."

"A bit like corruption in the police force," said Rachel grimly. "And there seems to be far too much of that if you ask me."

"So the stateroom steward was taking an unofficial bonus." Marjorie cackled.

"It's not funny," scolded Sarah.

"It's not the end of the world either, dear. Expensive jewellery should be locked in the safe or in the purser's office, so a few knick-knacks are hardly going to break the bank for the majority of passengers."

"It's not that, it's the breach of trust," argued Sarah.

"Sarah's right," said Rachel. "You need to be able to trust the crew."

"I've lived long enough to accept that isn't always possible, and when you remember the poverty many stewards leave behind in their homelands, it might be the temptation is too great. After all, cruise ships are the epitome of luxurious extravagance, aren't they?"

Rachel caught the naughty twinkle in Marjorie's eye, but could sense indignation building in Sarah so she felt it a good time to change the subject.

"Where do you suppose Dave Hughes was today?"

"I overheard one of the guys saying when they got back to the ship that he had a hangover and stayed behind, although the groom-to-be joked about it being funny that Tonya was also ill today."

"Ah," said Marjorie. "A secret liaison."

"Not that secret by the sounds of it," added Rachel.

They finished their pastries and teas before heading back to their respective rooms to change for dinner.

"I'm on call tonight, so I'll catch you tomorrow," said Sarah. "Let me know if you get anywhere with the Gordon thing, though."

"Will do," agreed Rachel as she kissed her friend on the cheek. "Where's Jason, by the way?"

"I'm not sure, working somewhere. He caught the jewellery thief," Sarah answered proudly.

Before Marjorie could say anything, Rachel took her arm and led her towards the lifts where they turned to wave to Sarah.

"I wasn't going to tease her any further, you know," Marjorie declared.

"Of course not." Rachel winked.

The next morning, Rachel and Marjorie split up to follow their respective action plans. Rachel stopped by Waverley's office after breakfast. The security chief looked chipper, radiating a newfound confidence.

"Good morning, Rachel. I just wanted to tell you we have dropped the investigation into Dominic Venables's death."

Open mouthed, Rachel found herself speechless.

"In the light of the drugs business and his general state, the company has, erm, advised me to rule out foul play from our end."

Rachel recognised what was happening. "How convenient," she said.

A momentary frown crossed the chief's face and Rachel suspected he was not altogether happy with this outcome either, but would have to toe the party line.

"As for the attack on Gordon Venables and yourself," he coughed, "that investigation continues. Our main line of inquiry is that it was one of the band, suspecting Gordon had killed their friend."

"What about Dave Hughes?"

"Unlikely. He would have been recovering from the assault on himself, so I don't think he would have gone near his uncle so soon afterwards."

"Does Gordon realise yet he has a nephew?"

"No, Mr Hughes doesn't want Gordon Venables told. He wants to put the whole thing behind him and get on with his life."

"Also convenient," Rachel murmured.

"Pardon?"

"Nothing. Did you find out when the new lead singer boarded?"

Waverley reached for a piece of paper on his desk. "A red herring, I'm afraid. Mr and Mrs Travers boarded on the afternoon of our arrival in Tallinn and moved to the crew quarters on deck A."

"The afternoon, you say? That can't be right. I saw them in the morning."

"You are mistaken, Rachel, they boarded at 3.30pm."

Rachel took out her mobile phone and pulled up the photo, placing the phone down deliberately on Waverley's desk.

"Is that a mistake, then?"

The furrowed brow showed confusion penetrating the previously happy face of the chief of security.

"When was this taken?"

"You can see from the time and date stamp, I snapped it on the morning in question, while you were speaking to the band members and before you spoke to me and Sarah."

He picked up her phone and enlarged the image with his fingers on the screen. He tapped names into his computer and pulled up the photos of the new lead singer and his wife. They both compared the images.

"Unless they are twin brothers married to twin sisters, I would say they are the same couple," said Rachel triumphantly.

Waverley slumped back in his chair. "I don't understand this at all. I will look into the matter, but it still has no bearing on the death of Dominic Venables. *Accidental* death."

"You can't believe that?" Rachel was astonished.

"I can and I do. Leave it with me – if I find out anything, I'll come back to you. It's probably a computer error on the boarding time, we do get the odd glitches in the system."

Rachel left, frustrated and angry.

"Insufferable arrogance of the man! Sheer blind stupidity."

This type of frustration was becoming a regular visitor to her life. Conversations with Carlos leapt into her mind about incidents at work where closing cases sometimes got in the way of finding the truth. Compromises she was uncomfortable with sprang up like a geyser ready to explode.

She found herself walking briskly towards her next destination, the determined look in her eyes a warning to anyone not to test her resolve. She would get to the bottom of the death of Dominic Venables, which was no more an accident than her being hit over the head and pushed into the pool. He may not have been a likeable character, and was apparently a junkie to boot, but that didn't mean his murderer shouldn't be brought to justice.

Rachel marched into the Sky View Lounge. The stag group happened to be participating in a marshmallow eating competition. Her indignation rose as she saw Gordon officiating.

This fiasco is getting worse.

Slamming herself down in a seat close to the front, she drew a nervous stare from a nearby couple. After taking a few deep calming breaths, she regained her composure and requested mineral water from a waiter, smiling reassuringly at the couple who tentatively looked away.

Her focus turned to the spectacle in front of her. The participants had to place as many marshmallows in their mouths as they could without chewing or swallowing, and the one who could hold the most at once was the winner. A few of them gave up fairly quickly and graciously accepted defeat, but the more competitive continued with the sickening display. Gordon and his assistant watched for any attempts at swallowing and Rachel noticed buckets nearby in case any of them threw up.

Gross!

Rachel could have gagged a few times herself in spite of having a fairly healthy stomach. The couple nearby retreated after the woman began to look a little green.

Gordon looked smug at being reinstated as cruise director and he gave Rachel a huge smile and a wave. Her smile hid the contempt she felt over his behaviour towards his wife – he had no idea she was aware – and her disgust that he had been allowed to go back to work as if nothing had happened after attacking one of the men now participating in the competition. Her smile was more at the irony of the situation.

It seemed Dave Hughes and the groom-to-be, Aled Lewis, were the most competitive because both looked about ready to regurgitate the contents of their mouths, and in all likelihood anything left in their stomachs, but neither would concede. Dave's face still had the bruises left from his previous meeting with Gordon and the latter was clearly enjoying adding to the young man's pain by encouraging him to take one more marshmallow. Just when it looked like both men would indeed vomit, Gordon's assistant hissed something in his ear and he brought proceedings to a close.

"Ladies and gentleman, in the name of decency, I declare it a draw."

Hugely relieved, the men turned away and spat the contents of their mouths into the waiting buckets, to the sound of cheers and jeers from their friends and amused passengers who had gathered to watch. Gordon awarded both men a lanyard with Queen Cruises Champion engraved on a plastic medallion and shook hands with them as if they were long-lost friends. Dave's eyes betrayed a steely cold gaze that sent chills down

Rachel's spine; she was sure she had her man.

Gordon quickly departed and left the gang of young men to their back-slapping and congratulatory teasing, each jostling to be heard above the other. Dave Hughes looked pale as he approached Rachel.

"Hi," he said warily. "The security bloke said you wanted to have a word with me. He told me you saved my bacon the other day by the side of the pool."

Rachel slapped her most disarming smile on to her face as she encouraged him to take a seat.

"Catch you later, boys," he shouted to his mates.

"Lucky blighter," one of them remarked. "What do they see in him?"

"I'm Rachel." She had rehearsed the next part of her speech with Marjorie until it sounded convincing. "I witnessed the assault on you the other day, and wanted to tell you that I am happy to make a formal complaint about the whole thing to the security team to ensure that man never works again."

He looked nervous. "No!" He raised his voice and Rachel feigned alarm, moving away from him.

"Sorry, I didn't mean to shout. It's just the whole thing has been traumatic for me. I want to forget about it. In fact, I've already told the chief to drop it."

"Really? I'm surprised, are you sure that's wise? That man shouldn't be allowed to get away with what he did to you. He's even back at work – rubbing your face in it, that's what I'd call it."

The hatred in Dave's eyes gave him away again, but he quickly regained control.

"It was nothing. In fact, it was a family spat. Don't tell anyone, but he's my uncle, and I deserved it. Don't worry, I'll get him back." The malice became evident in his voice during the latter part of the statement. Rachel wanted to rattle his cage a little bit more.

"That's very forgiving of you, but it was still assault, uncle or not. I'll tell the chief I want to make a formal statement."

Rachel moved as if to leave. He gripped her arm aggressively, his eyes pleading.

"No, please, don't – you'll ruin everything."

"But he has to be dealt with," she said sympathetically. "People like him should be punished. In fact, I'd like to do it myself."

"What do you mean?" he asked.

"Well if it was left to me, I'd throw him overboard."

The young man's eyes welled up. "My dad was thrown overboard."

"I'm so sorry, I didn't realise. Was your dad that superb singer in the Queen tribute band?"

"Yes." He looked down at his clenched fists. "And I intend to get the killer."

"OMG! You think it was your uncle?"

"I know it was, so you have to understand, he will be punished, but the security chief's told me they don't suspect him of murder, so if he gets arrested he'll only get done for assault. Don't you see? He'll get away with murder."

"What are you going to do?"

"I can't tell you. I nearly got to him the other day, but he survived." He looked determined. "Next time I'll make sure."

Rachel was puzzled he hadn't recognised her as the person who shouted at him to leave the man alone, but relieved to see Jason come into the lounge. Her plan had worked – she'd got the confession.

"I'm sorry, Mr Hughes, I can't let you do that." Dave's eyes darted from Rachel to Jason, who was approaching them. "There's nowhere to run."

Rachel took the phone out of her pocket and handed it to Jason. "Everything's on there, but please let me have it back ASAP. I'm expecting a call."

Before Jason led Dave Hughes away, Rachel spoke to the young man.

"Believe me," she said, "attempted murder is better than committing the real thing. You're too young to go away for life, and if it helps, I'm almost certain it wasn't your uncle that killed your dad."

Dave looked back at her. "So you think it was drugs that killed him?"

"Perhaps, but if there is a killer, I don't believe it's Gordon Venables. He doesn't have it in him."

"Who are you?"

"Just someone trying to enjoy a holiday." She shrugged as Jason took the young man away. "And oh how I wish I could do that."

Chapter 28

Marjorie arrived in the main atrium in plenty of time for her meeting with Jimmy Walker. She ordered tea and sat gazing out to sea through the large windows that allowed torrents of light into the area. The marble floors shone with polish, as did the spiral staircases leading to the upper part of the atrium. The brass banisters were so shiny they could be used as mirrors.

If one sat here all day long, she mused, *one would see the invisible crew who keep the public areas immaculately clean and tidy.*

The public toilets were a perfect example. She had never known a time when soap or towels were lacking. Spillages were magically cleaned up immediately by a member of the crew who no-one noticed or acknowledged. The daily routine continued like the well-oiled machine it was. Rigorous training kept the crew on their toes, Sarah had assured her and Rachel, with work regularly inspected by senior officers throughout every department.

The atrium was busy, being a sea day. The cruisers had had four straight days of land stops and now they were enjoying the hospitality the ship had to offer before the next stop. Marjorie had finished her first cup of tea before the band manager arrived. He came alone at first as per her request, with the rest of the band due half an hour later.

The loud voice shattered her musings. "Allo, Lady Snellforpe, good to see ya again."

I do wish he would learn some diction. He can say 'the', so why can't he say 'thorpe'?

"Good morning, Mr Walker. I trust you enjoyed some relaxation over the past few days. Tea?"

"I'll 'ave coffee, ta."

Marjorie requested coffee from the waiter, who had seen Jimmy arrive, and another pot of tea for herself.

"The lads went ashore while I worked. Never a minute's rest, managing a band, what wiv bookings and rooms and making sure they've got everyfing they need."

"Yes, I'm sure it's a full-time job. You do seem to manage them well, though. My granddaughter liked the new singer, but not as much as the previous one, she told me."

Jimmy's jaw dropped.

"However, she's willing to have another listen when they play this afternoon, and afterwards I will make my final decision. It is such a shame about Mr Venables."

"Well, as I said, 'e could be difficult at times wiv 'is temperament an' all, plus the fact men couldn't let their wives out of their sight. Like I told ya, 'e even 'ad a go at mine."

"Quite. I still can't get over how forgiving you were over that incident; it must have riled you. My late husband would not have shown so much grace."

Marjorie noticed Jimmy fiddling with his collar as the memories came back. "Yeah, well, as I said, I was angry and could 'ave done for 'im the day I found out, but we made up. In business, you 'ave to let things go. We needed each other and 'e promised it wouldn't 'appen again, like."

"Artistic people do sometimes push all social boundaries, don't they?"

"Yeah, they can do, I suppose." He took a slurp of coffee from the mug that had arrived while they chatted. Marjorie

thanked the waiter, but Jimmy didn't
seem to notice him at all.

And he'd be the first to call me a snob.

For a moment, she was distracted by the
loud slurping noises he made as his jaw
performed somersaults to keep the gum in
place while drinking.

"Do they know yet who done for him,
as you put it?"

"They don't fink anyone did now. Last
I 'eard they put it down to an accident.
Now saying 'e was drunk and off 'is 'ead
on drugs." He snorted in disbelief.

"You don't think it an accident, I take
it?"

"Dom was a lot of fings, but a junkie
ain't one of 'em. 'E never touched the
'ard stuff; a bit of pot now and again, but
not what they say 'e took."

"What do they say he took?"

"LSD! Lady Snellforpe, the lads are
clean, they don't do drugs, and Dom

always warned them off such stuff. Said if they needed those kinds of drugs to be creative, they weren't good enough to work wiv." Jimmy's voice rose a few decibels and people stared at him, although he remained oblivious. He waved his hands in the air and chewed harder on his gum as if to prove the point. "My lads are clean."

Deciding to bring him back down from the ceiling, Marjorie suggested ordering drinks for the imminent arrival of 'his lads'. He recovered himself and she imagined how exhausting it must be to have a volatile temperament – up one minute, down the next. She couldn't see the point. People might criticise the stoical British temperament, but she would take that any day rather than the constant roller coaster ride many seemed to live by these days.

Maybe I am too old, she pondered while Jimmy rattled on about contracts and costs and bookings. Her attention returned when he stopped speaking and looked at her, obviously waiting for an answer to a question she hadn't caught.

Seeing the open diary in his hand, she guessed.

"We'll need to wait until this afternoon for that."

He slammed the diary shut, disappointed. Relieved at having guessed the right answer, Marjorie realised she was tired and wished Rachel had accompanied her. This investigating business might be all well and good, but she was not used to dealing with people like Walker.

Chastising herself for her weakness, she concentrated on the job in hand as the rest of the band made their entrance heard and approached the table.

"I was just telling Lady Snellforpe 'ow you don't do drugs, boys."

"Too right we don't," said Nick. "And I don't believe Dom did either."

Marjorie would have counted 'pot', as Walker called it, as a drug, but didn't want to split hairs. They obviously believed there was a distinction between what they did and drugs.

"You can't argue with what they found at autopsy," said Ray.

"I'm sure he did all sorts of things we didn't have a clue about," said Dalton.

"Oh, don't start again, Dalton. Come out of cuckoo land for a bit, won't you?" Nick hissed.

Dalton blushed and stared down at his shoes. Marjorie sympathised with him; he seemed a sensitive sort and the constant bickering must wear him down.

No wonder he seeks attention through fantasy.

Jimmy turned to the new lead singer who had a woman hanging on to his arm. He had short ginger hair and a moustache, presumably to resemble Freddie Mercury. His hair was unmistakable from the photo Rachel had shown her and Sarah a few days earlier.

"This is Fred and Millie."

"Fred as in Freddie Mercury?" Marjorie enquired.

"Ironic, isn't it?" Fred didn't have the cockney accent most of the band shared. "It is my real name. Inevitable I would play him, I was named after him. My parents' fault, huge fans."

"Oh, did you play Freddie Mercury before with the band?"

His jawline became jagged as he answered. "No, I should have been lead singer, but the venerable Dom Venables took over not long after we started out." He glared at the rest of the band. "And what a mistake that turned out to be," he added.

With so much testosterone flying about, it's a wonder they ever got anything done.

"But he's our leading man now, eh?" Jimmy interjected, trying to divert the conversation.

"Dom got his comeuppance." Fred was not to be dissuaded that easily.

"Now, now, Fred – let's not talk ill of the dead."

"I don't see why not," Nick argued. "No point pretending he was anything but bad news – we could have been famous now if it weren't for him holding us back."

"Come on, Nick, that was never gonna happen," said Ray, who seemed to be the only person satisfied with his lot.

"We don't know that – we should have made our own music, not lost our identity being a stupid tribute act."

"I agree," said Fred. "We used to make our own music until the esteemed Dom joined and convinced these losers to be a tribute. He actually thought he might be Freddie Mercury reincarnated – it's laughable. For a start, they happened to be alive at the same time – Mercury died in 1991 and Dom was born in 1969. Do the maths!"

"I never thought of that," said Dalton.

The rest stared at him in disbelief.

Not the shiniest tool in the box.

Marjorie chuckled inwardly, but at least it brought about a change of subject as the rest of the group teased Dalton mercilessly over his faux pas.

Rachel and Marjorie met up and compared notes before arranging to see Waverley in his office prior to lunch. They found him whistling a tune as they arrived. His door was wide open.

Marjorie nudged Rachel. "I told you he's in love," she whispered.

Waverley turned just in time to catch the two women sniggering. He looked confused, but didn't comment.

"Come in, ladies, take a seat."

They sat on the sofa and he took one of the soft chairs opposite.

"First, I need to thank you, Rachel. We have a full confession from Dave Hughes. He said he attacked his uncle and you – although he didn't realise it was you – and it appears *we* were right about Dominic Venables. He was murdered – Dave's confessed to that murder too."

Waverley beamed from ear to ear while rubbing his hands together. Marjorie gasped and Rachel remained silent.

Waverley explained how Hughes had said he'd got angry with his father for ignoring him on board ship, they'd had a row. Venables was drunk, Hughes punched him and walked away. Later, he realised he must have punched him too hard and his father staggered and fell.

"Manslaughter rather than murder. He didn't realise he'd killed him."

"So why attack Gordon?" asked Marjorie.

"Revenge for humiliating him on the lido deck, he decided he'd get his own back. You're quiet, Rachel, I thought you'd be pleased – another case solved by PC Prince."

"Sorry, I find it hard to believe, particularly as he sounded pretty convinced that Gordon had murdered his father when I spoke to him this morning. He clearly stated he held Gordon responsible and threatened to kill him, or words to that effect, although I think it's all bravado. He may well have punched his father, but the coroner said Venables had been hit from behind before the neat drug scenario changed everyone's minds.

"In fact, I now don't think Dave attacked Gordon at all, or me. It hasn't sat right since I spoke to Dave this morning. He didn't have the facts and didn't give the impression someone else – namely me – had been attacked at the same time. He was terrified when Gordon attacked him by the lido pool – I can see why he wants people to think he's brave and vengeful, but he's just a big pussycat trying to be macho in front of his mates."

"You're the one who had us arrest him."

"Yes I did, but now I'm not so sure. It might play into our hands, though, so we can catch the real perpetrator. Did Dave volunteer that he'd attacked me or did you ask him?"

The other two stared in confusion at Rachel, Waverley groaning and brushing back the imaginary hair from his forehead.

"Now you mention it, I asked him. Why didn't you tell me this was a ruse?"

"To be honest, it wasn't, but the longer I spoke to Dave Hughes, the more I felt in my gut it wasn't him. He's just an insecure young man whose dream of being reunited with the father who abandoned him and his mother died a death. It's like he's now trying to be the bad man like his father."

"Great psychology, Rachel," said Waverley disparagingly. "Where's the evidence – apart from your gut, of course?"

"Now, Chief, sarcasm doesn't become you, and I for one am a great believer in Rachel's gut," said Marjorie, taking Rachel's hand protectively.

Waverley groaned again just as there was a knock on the door.

"COME IN!" he bellowed.

Jason entered the office accompanied by the groom-to-be from the stag group and Sarah.

"Sorry to interrupt, sir, but you should hear what this lad has to say. This is Aled Lewis, best friend of Dave Hughes."

Waverley glared but gathered his composure. "Come and sit down, Mr Lewis, we meet at last. Your party has caused us quite a few problems."

Rachel and Marjorie exchanged glances with Sarah who took a seat with them on the sofa. Aled sat on the other soft chair while Jason remained standing. The young man looked sheepish.

"Sorry about that, sir, the boys do get carried away when they've had a few." His Welsh lilt and smile were disarming. "I've just heard about Davey's confession so I came immediately. He couldn't have attacked that cruise director – he was in our room with me. He'd drunk too much, and while he was thrashing about in bed, he cut his head open again, you see. I called the medics and this nurse came and glued his head."

"Is this true, Sarah?" asked Waverley.

"Yes. I checked the records, and they called me at 5am. I left their room at around 6am after being summoned to attend to Gordon Venables and Rachel."

"I don't suppose you were around when Dave punched his father?" Waverley asked Aled.

"As a matter of fact, I was, but Davey doesn't know that. He kept ranting about how his dad left his mother, how he'd hero worshipped the man – famous singer and all that. He's always been impressionable. Anyway, he flew off the handle, miffed that the man had been ignoring him since he'd told him he was on board and determined to have it out with him. He stormed out of the room. I followed to make sure he didn't do anything stupid because he'd had a few, like. Anyway, I saw the confrontation they had. His dad was horrible to him and told him to grow up – he wasn't the daddy type – and to go back to his whore of a mother. Davey did lose it and punched him. The guy was so drunk he reeled back and Davey stormed off. I stayed to see if the bloke was alright."

"And was he?" Rachel found herself holding her breath.

"He was fine, laughing out loud. Called Davey a few names under his breath, then lit up a cigarette as if nothing had happened. He walked unevenly over to the ship's rail and started yelling at the world what a great man he was. I returned to our room to check on Davey, but I never told him what I'd seen – he would have been gutted to know anyone had witnessed how dismissive his great hero dad had been."

"You're a good friend to have," said Sarah.

"Thanks," said Aled blushing.

"Thank you, Mr Lewis, for telling us. I need you to keep this to yourself for now because we want the real murderer and attacker of our cruise director to imagine they are safe. Do you understand?"

"Yes, sir. Will you be letting Davey go?"

"We'll hang on to him for now. I don't want his anger to spill over into actually doing something silly, and it will add to the real attacker's belief that he is safe." Waverley nodded to Jason to take Aled outside and record what he'd just said.

After they'd left, Waverley looked at Rachel.

"Right again, Miss Prince."

"Sorry," she said.

"So," he sighed, "we're back to square one."

"Not really," said Rachel. "We've narrowed the field and we're getting closer to finding out which one of the band is involved. As you say, whoever it is will feel safe now, and for whatever reason, they want Gordon Venables out of the way. I assume you've got a tail on him?"

"How did you know?"

"My gut!" They all laughed, including Waverley. "I knew you would need a better reason for letting him go back to work than blind belief in his innocence."

"He's agreed to be bait as long as he keeps his job if proven innocent, which is quite brave of him under the circumstances. I almost called off the watch, but I'm glad I didn't. We will catch whoever it is trying to kill him."

"What if they don't try again?" asked Sarah. "And worse, what if they do and they succeed?"

"I agree," said Rachel. "We need to work out the motive for a double murder – if we do that, we find the killer. Marjorie and I are meeting the band and the manager this afternoon. I'm hoping we'll find out something. They all seem to have hated Dom, but I don't understand why any of them would want to kill Gordon."

"And you're sure it's one of them?" asked Waverley.

"Ninety-nine per cent certain that one of them killed Dom Venables, and for some reason, now wants to kill his brother."

"What if it's all of them?" asked Marjorie. "Remember I joked about *Murder on the Orient Express* – what if they hated him so much they planned this together?"

"That is a possibility." Waverley scratched his head. "Horrendous as it may seem."

"We will probably find out today," said Rachel.

"Do be careful, Rachel, and you, Marjorie."

"Don't worry, my dear," said Marjorie, "I won't let her out of my sight."

"I'm not sure that's very reassuring." Sarah laughed. "The pair of you are as bad as each other."

"We'll continue the watch on Gordon and I will have one of my men hanging around when you meet with the band. Do you want to wear a wire?"

"I'll record on the mobile if you can give it back to me."

"Yes, we've taken what we need." Waverley walked behind his desk and took the mobile from it.

Rachel took her phone back and quickly checked for messages in case of any word from Carlos. Disappointed she returned her gaze to Waverley. "They won't try anything this afternoon, but I'm hoping they'll talk enough to give something away. Marjorie's going to be very generous with the spirits during our meeting."

The two women exchanged conspiratorial glances as they rose to leave.

Chapter 29

The fishing expedition with the band had
been totally unproductive in terms of
discovering anything new. They happened
to be their usual argumentative selves, but
Jimmy seemed determined to stick to his
objective of getting Marjorie to book
them for Rachel's imaginary birthday
party later in the year. Each time Marjorie
or Rachel tried to steer the conversation
towards the death of the late lead singer,
Jimmy interrupted, preventing anyone
from pursuing the subject any further. In
the end, Marjorie provisionally booked
them just to convince Jimmy that they
were genuine. Then, feigning tiredness,
she said she would finalise details after
her port outing the next day.

"It's as if he did that deliberately,"
Rachel complained.

"If he did, he's onto us. We should proceed with caution."

"There's only one thing for it now – my Plan B, which Waverley would not agree to."

"What's that?"

"I need to go through their cabins while they're performing tonight. Waverley said there was no justification when I suggested it earlier – not enough evidence against them."

"Why didn't I think of that? What a good idea – we'll go together."

"Oh no, Marjorie, I can't ask you to go down there, it's too dangerous. The stairs are steep, metallic and difficult to negotiate, the rooms are tiny, and no offence, but you'd stick out like a sore thumb. Besides, I need you to keep an eye on the band and send me warning if any of them disappear during their break."

"You can't go alone. Take Sarah with you."

"No, I almost got her in trouble the last time I ventured down to the crew cabins. Besides, she's on call and I can't have her radio going off when I'm on a secret mission."

They discussed the plan back in Marjorie's suite before dinner. Rachel bought walkie-talkies from the on-board gift shop and showed Marjorie how to use hers if she needed to warn her about anything. Marjorie was thoroughly enjoying herself. Rachel apologised to the old lady for having to subject her to another evening of loud pop music, but even that didn't put her off.

"If anyone thinks it strange I'm there, I'll stick to the hiring them for a party story."

What they needed to do now was get hold of a universal swipe key and Rachel knew just where to find one. Waverley carried spares in the top right-hand drawer of his desk – she had seen them when he'd offered her a job in the past. Their problem consisted of how to get into his room without him realising.

Marjorie and Rachel decided to pay him an unannounced visit to explain that they had got nowhere with the band, sharing their frustration. He took it all in and sighed.

"An update on the new singer, by the way: it appears he and his wife did board earlier on the day in question. A computer update caused a temporary glitch that has now corrected itself. And now that security has less to do, I can't ask you to continue your involvement, so leave it to my team. Thank you for your assistance."

Rachel nodded before Marjorie could protest.

"Good idea. We're on holiday, aren't we, Marjorie?"

"Yes indeed. Have you spoken to that young man yet, Chief?"

"I was just about to go when you two ladies arrived, so if you'll excuse me." He stood up.

Perfect, thought Rachel as he walked them out. Just as they were leaving, Marjorie tripped, causing Waverley to rush forwards to support her.

"Are you alright, Lady Snellthorpe?"

"Yes, silly old thing that I am. I do lose my footing occasionally these days."

"Sit down for a moment, Marjorie. I'll get you a glass of water. Don't worry about us, Chief, you go ahead." Rachel smiled encouragingly.

"If you're sure? I would like to speak to Hughes, and then I've got to join the captain's table for some paying dinner guests."

"Quite sure," said Marjorie. "You go along, I am quite alright."

As soon as he was out of sight, Marjorie looked at Rachel.

"Did you manage it?"

"Like taking candy from a baby." After checking the coast was clear, Rachel crossed the corridor back to Waverley's office where she had inserted a piece of card to prevent the door locking while the distraction caused by Marjorie diverted his attention.

"Stay put, and if anyone comes along, pretend you're waiting for someone."

"Strictly speaking, I am." Marjorie laughed.

Rachel entered the office and prayed he hadn't locked his drawers. She crossed the room quickly and crouched down on hands and knees – because he'd left the blinds open, she couldn't risk being seen. Her heart was pounding and hands were trembling by the time she got to the other side of his desk. Reaching up, she pulled the drawer to find it was locked.

Drat and blast. All this for nothing. Lock picking wasn't her forté.

She sat on the floor, trying to work out what to do next. Risking raising her head up, she peeked at what was on top of the desk. Minimalistic order was his thing: the desk top consisted of a computer, the keyboard and a photo of a pretty girl about Rachel's age who in all likelihood was his daughter. The desk-tidy gave her a surge of hope, but on checking if he'd dropped his keys in there, she found nothing.

About to give up, she spotted a shelf of books to the right of the desk. A small silver tin sat at one end. Again risking being seen, she stood up, quickly checking the corridor for people. A couple walked past with their backs to her as she grabbed the tin and slunk back down to the floor.

The tin was embossed with faux ivory, something Waverley had probably picked up in Asia. As Rachel removed the lid, her eyes lit up with delight at the sight of a small set of keys.

With her heart beating ever faster, she tried each key in the lock. On the third attempt, the lock clicked. Her hands were shaking almost out of control as she pulled the drawer open, grabbed a lanyard with a universal swipe card on it, and closed and locked the drawer, panting.

Raising herself up off the floor, she felt dread return on seeing Waverley heading in her direction. Panic set in as she saw him stop to speak to Marjorie. Then he turned and walked in the opposite direction, giving her the opportunity to quickly replace the tin and race across the room and out the door.

Breathless, she sat down next to Marjorie.

"What kept you? I was so worried."

"The drawer was locked, I had to find a key. How did you get rid of Waverley?"

"I told him I was worried about you as you hadn't returned with my water and sent him off in the direction you never went in. I think we'd better leave."

They bumped into Waverley in the midships area. "I was concerned. Where were you?" he said to Rachel.

"Sorry, I got caught short, and then bumped into Mario, our butler, and we got chatting. All's good now." Deceit didn't come naturally and Rachel crossed her fingers behind her back. Waverley seemed satisfied and headed back to his office to collect whatever it was he'd forgotten.

"There's only one downside to this plan, you know," said Marjorie.

"What's that?" asked Rachel.

"You'll be on CCTV."

Rachel slapped her head. "You're right. Let's hope they don't have any reason to check it tonight. After that, I'll own up if need be and take the consequences. If not, I can easily put the key back."

"How?"

Rachel waved the lanyard. "I have a key!"

As they walked arm in arm towards the restaurant for dinner, no-one would have imagined what they had planned for the rest of the evening.

Chapter 30

Rachel joined Marjorie in the Culture Lounge. The surprised look on her elderly friend's face made her laugh.

There was little chance they could converse above the noise of the band, by now in full swing belting out *Bohemian Rhapsody*, the delighted passengers reliving their seventies' memories by throwing themselves around the dance floor, much to the chagrin of the younger members of their families. One man in particular appeared to be getting a little carried away.

"He'll do himself a mischief if he's not careful," shouted Marjorie.

"Or someone else, most likely. Come on, let's go somewhere quiet, I've got news for you."

They left the bass behind and made their way to the main atrium where a string quartet was playing a mixture of Vivaldi and Mozart.

"Now this is much more my cup of tea!" exclaimed Marjorie.

"That's what I love about cruising, there's so much variety, something for every taste."

"What happened? You were too quick to have been through all the rooms."

"I got lucky," Rachel said triumphantly. "I know what's going on."

After she had explained her findings to Marjorie and her suspicions, they agreed the time had come to involve Waverley and set a trap. Rachel asked guest services to call the chief of security as a matter of urgency and she and Marjorie waited for him to arrive.

He looked a little flushed as he made his way over to their table, conveniently situated behind a large pillar but in full view of the small dance floor and a stage where the quartet continued to produce aesthetic sounds. Rachel looked closely at the chief and wondered if he had been drinking, or whether the post prandial exercise had caused his face to burn brightly.

He sounded sober enough when he sat down. "Good evening again, ladies. I was informed you needed to see me urgently." His curtness told them they had obviously interrupted something important – a date?

Rachel smiled. "Sorry to disturb you, but yes, it is urgent." She explained her discovery, neatly omitting to mention how she'd acquired a key card. Thankfully, Waverley seemed more concerned with the gravity of the situation and the shock revelation than with her method. "I have a flytrap plan, but we will need Gordon's cooperation to carry it out," said Rachel finally.

Waverley listened intently, only asking pertinent questions, and immediately sprang into action.

"Follow me," he instructed while speaking into his radio, requesting Gordon to come to his office along with two security officers.

Gordon tentatively agreed to the plan and left them to set proceedings in motion. They needed to wait until eleven-thirty, but set themselves up fifteen minutes before, moving to the bow of the ship and hiding themselves in the theatre where Gordon would be arranging his meeting. Although Rachel would have preferred Marjorie to wait in Waverley's office, she insisted on attending.

"I don't want to miss the action now we've got this far," the older lady insisted.

In the dark, Rachel could hear Waverley's breathing and imagined him sweating. He had the most to lose if this trap turned horribly wrong – second to Gordon, that was.

After what seemed an age they heard footsteps walking on to the stage, followed by shuffling as someone hid themselves. Rachel's heart was pounding with anticipation and she prayed their plan would work.

Silence ensued for what seemed an eternity, but in reality could only have been around five minutes. No-one dared move for fear of alerting the person hiding on stage. At one point, a couple mistakenly entered the theatre from the back, giggled at finding themselves in the wrong place and left again.

The silence became deafening and Rachel could feel her muscles stiffening with tension from the hunched position in her hiding place. She hoped Marjorie would be alright – she had ensured the old lady was in a more comfortable hiding place than the one she'd found for herself. Just beginning to wonder if Gordon had changed his mind and chickened out, Rachel heard footsteps approaching and saw someone shining a torch.

A commotion occurred and the man dropped the torch and grunted as if someone had attacked him.

Waverley flicked on the lights and shouted, "That's enough – the game's up. Let him go."

The dastardly duo on the stage looked stunned at having been caught in the act. Gordon sat on the floor with his head in his hands.

"I suppose you were going to say your husband attacked you and you hit him in self-defence," said Rachel to Shirley Venables, now handcuffed and held by a security officer. Dalton Delacruz was also in cuffs.

"How did you find out?"

"When I took that photo of you and Sarah in Tallinn, I remembered catching a brief glimpse of a photo of you with a man. At first, I assumed it was Gordon, but it came to me earlier this evening that it could have been someone else, someone I recognised. Tonight while you were performing, I slipped into the changing rooms backstage and found your phone with your clothes. I was grateful you used a combination of your date of birth as a pass code – not wise, by the way. I checked the photo, and sure enough, you and Dalton were in a lover's embrace. What I didn't understand was why you had Dominic killed or why you didn't just leave Gordon and take up with Dalton. But it was all about money, wasn't it?"

Gordon looked at Rachel, clearly unable to look at his wife. "Who killed my brother?"

"Dalton, under instructions from your wife, I'm afraid. Dom had seen them together and threatened to tell you unless she came clean with you herself. He hadn't tried it on with her at all – he really was trying to mend his ways as far as you were concerned. Dalton knew they had been seen by a passenger – Dave Hughes, as it turned out – so he made up a story about Shirley and Dom to throw everyone off the scent. Even though he wouldn't be believed entirely, it muddied the waters enough to draw suspicion away from him. Shirley convinced Dalton she would run away with him, but didn't want to lose out on her inheritance with you still alive. I think she played Dalton to get at your money. He'd do the dirty work, she would be very rich, and later she'd dump him."

"Why did he pretend he had tried it on with Shirley when I confronted him?" asked Gordon, confused.

"Old habits die hard, I guess," answered Rachel.

"I suspected she was having an affair. I told her I was going to change my will, so I guess that's what brought on the urgency."

"I'm afraid so," said Rachel, putting a hand on Gordon's shoulder. "You were never the controlling one in the relationship, either. Jealous yes, but controlling, no. Your wife had everyone convinced you were a psychological abuser. It was the other way round."

Gordon, horrified, finally looked at his wife. "Why would you say that? They told me I had to stay away from you because you wanted to leave me."

Shirley glared at him. "You're pathetic, Gordon. Always in your brother's shadow. I only married you when I discovered you'd made a small fortune from developing a stupid app, but cautious Gordon would never spend any money. Saving it for a rainy day! I might as well have married a pauper."

"So the only way of getting your hands on the money was by killing your husband. What a callous woman you are." Marjorie's voice betrayed her disgust.

"Humph," said Shirley.

"Who sent the letter?" asked Waverley.

"She sent it to herself. Am I right?" asked Rachel.

"It seemed a good idea and kept the security team off the scent."

"What I don't understand," said Marjorie, "is why Mr Delacruz would agree to murder someone on your behalf so soon after you met?"

"I don't think they had just met," Rachel explained, looking at Shirley. "You were never really kept locked away in Wales, were you?"

"No, we met up with the band whenever they were in Cardiff. Dalton and I had a fling then."

"So my suspicions were right about you having affairs?" Gordon looked at his wife in astonishment.

Ignoring him, Shirley looked at Waverley. "I did wonder why you allowed my husband back to work."

"Mr Hughes withdrew his complaint and I didn't have your husband down as a killer," said Waverley. "You nearly got away with it as Hughes had punched his father after an argument and later thought he was responsible for Dominic's death –

he even tried to take the rap for the attack on your husband."

Gordon looked astonished. "His father? What do you mean?"

"Yes, Gordon. Dom had a son who he abandoned at birth: Dave Hughes, the man you attacked. He really had seen a band member kissing your wife, but it was Dalton, not Dom." Rachel put a hand on his arm.

Gordon cried, "I'm so sorry, I don't know what came over me. I was in a jealous rage – a nephew? At least I have something left of Dom."

"See? You're pathetic!" spat Shirley scornfully.

"Take her away," commanded Waverley.

Dalton, who had been quiet until now, said, "She does love me, she told me."

"You were being used, man. Take him away too," ordered Waverley.

"So it was Dalton who tried to drown me?" asked Gordon.

"Yes, but he ran when I came along. It was Shirley who hit me – she was probably acting as a lookout, or perhaps she didn't trust Dalton to do the job properly."

"As I said," remarked Marjorie, "not the shiniest tool in the box."

Gordon looked a broken man as he walked away, shaking his head.

"He'll be alright," said Waverley. "We'll help him."

After the excitement had subsided and Waverley had left them, Rachel walked Marjorie to her room and kissed her on the cheek.

"Sleep tight, we've got a busy day touring tomorrow."

"You didn't get to use that security key below stairs then?"

"Not this time, but who knows? Maybe next time. Goodnight, Marjorie."

"Goodnight, Rachel."

Chapter 31

Two days later, a ringing in the distance penetrated Rachel's deep sleep. Coming round, she recognised the ringtone immediately and leapt out of bed, grabbing the phone in the sitting room and pressing the button.

"Carlos!"

"Hello, darling, did I wake you?"

Her eyes filled with tears of joy at the sound of his voice. "I can't think of a better way to be awoken." She clutched the phone tightly. "I was so worried. Are you back home?"

"Yes, another case solved by PI Jacobi. It was a lot more complicated than I'd thought – I'll tell you all about it when you get back. Lady was the star of the day, but I'm trying not to let her know that. She already has me wrapped around her paw."

"Oh Carlos, it's so good to hear your voice."

"Yours too, I've missed you. How is the cruise? I hope it has been relaxing."

"Erm, I think I'll tell you all about it when I get back."

"Oh?"

"Don't worry, it's all over now, but I'll give you all the details in London. We'll compare notes."

"I'll settle for that over dinner. Just tell me you and Marjorie are alright."

"We're fine. In fact, I'm pleased you woke me because we're getting an early train to Berlin today. It's our final stop."

"Enjoy that beautiful city. I'll join the chauffeur on Sunday to collect you; I'm taking a few days off myself after the events of the past ten days."

"That will be wonderful, I can't wait."

"Rachel," he sounded serious, "I should have said this a long time ago. I'm sorry if you don't want to hear it, but I love you."

She thought her heart would burst, knowing that he wouldn't say it unless he meant it. They had never said the words before, in spite of dating for almost two years.

"I love you too, Carlos."

"Then I'm the happiest man alive. See you on Sunday. *Ciao*."

When she collected Marjorie, Rachel was glowing.

"I take it you've heard from your beau." The twinkle in Marjorie's eye told her she understood all about love.

"He's accompanying Johnson on Sunday to collect us. I hope you don't mind?"

"I couldn't be more pleased. He's a good man and he loves you, you know."

"I know that now."

They met up with Sarah in the main atrium before leaving the ship to take the train into Berlin. The three women had lots to tell each other as so much had happened, and Sarah had worked solidly the day after the arrests while Marjorie and Rachel were exploring Poland. Sarah told them Dave Hughes had been released and that he and his uncle were getting acquainted. Gordon was determined to forge a special bond with his nephew and make up for the lack of support his brother had provided.

"Oh, I am pleased," said Marjorie. "I do believe they will be good for each other and may be able to provide the solace needed for healing to take place."

"I think you're right there," agreed Sarah. "I liked Gordon until his darker side threatened to overwhelm him. I do hope he learns to rid himself of that temper."

"Let's hope he can get help to recover from the wounds his brother and his wife have inflicted on him," said Marjorie thoughtfully. "The fact his brother was on his side in the end might help him heal."

"On the subject of Shirley Venables, Waverley told me yesterday he'd had a report back from their previous ship. Shirley had a fling with a fellow dancer and had to have treatment for a sexually transmitted disease. The report had been marked confidential to prevent Gordon finding out. The doctor suggested she make up a story about problems with her contraceptive implant to prevent Gordon catching it while she was treated. He still doesn't know."

"My, my, she had me fooled," said Rachel.

"Not only you," said Marjorie kindly.

"On a lighter note, the other news on the *Coral* grapevine is that Waverley's got engaged! Bernard overheard Graham congratulating him this morning."

"I told you so," said Marjorie triumphantly.

"That is good news." Rachel was happy for him.

"Will you cruise again, Rachel, or has this put you off for life?" asked Sarah.

"On the contrary, I get more experience on this cruise ship than I do in the police force. I very much look forward to cruising again in the summer. I have been offered a rather large compensation sum once again following the attack on board your beloved ship."

Sarah's eyes lit up. "I'm so pleased, I love seeing you during my contracts. It reminds me of home."

"I enjoy the travel too, despite the criminals you get on your ships. I've seen places I would never have dreamed of visiting. The St Petersburg ballet is up there with one of my best experiences to date."

"You've got the cruise bug, dear," said Marjorie happily.

The trio joined hands over the table and toasted each other with a mug of tea.

"To more cruises in the future," said Rachel as they clinked mugs.

"Preferably with proper china teacups!" Marjorie added, to which the girls laughed loudly.

THE END

Author's Note

Thank you for reading *Killer Cruise*, the third book in my Rachel Prince Mystery series. If you have enjoyed it, please leave an honest review on Amazon and/or any other platform you may use. I love receiving feedback from readers and can assure you that I read every review.

Keep an eye out for Book 4 in the *Rachel Prince Mystery* series. *Dying to Cruise* is due for release in summer 2019. Book 5 *A Christmas Cruise Caper* will be released in the autumn.

Keep in touch:

Signup for my no spam newsletter at: www.dawnbrookespublishing.com

Follow me on Facebook:
https://www.facebook.com/dawnbrookesp
ublishing/

Follow me on Twitter:
@dawnbrookes1

Follow me on Pinterest:
https://www.pinterest.co.uk/dawnbrookes
publishing/

About the Author

Dawn Brookes is author of the *Rachel Prince Mystery* series, combining a unique blend of murder, cruising and medicine with a touch of romance.

Dawn has a 39-year nursing pedigree and takes regular cruise holidays, which she says are for research purposes! She brings these passions together with a love of clean crime to her writing.

The surname of her protagonist is in honour of her childhood dog, Prince, who used to put his head on her knee while she lost herself in books.

Bestselling author of *Hurry up Nurse: memoirs of nurse training in the 1970s* and *Hurry up Nurse 2: London calling,*

Dawn worked as a hospital nurse, midwife, district nurse and community matron across her career. Before turning her hand to writing for a living, she had multiple articles published in professional journals and co-edited a nursing textbook.

She grew up in Leicester, later moved to London and Berkshire, but now lives in Derbyshire. Dawn holds a Bachelor's degree with Honours and a Master's degree in education. Writing across genres, she also writes for children. Dawn has a passion for nature and loves animals, especially dogs. Animals will continue to feature in her children's books as she believes caring for animals and nature helps children to become kinder human beings.

Acknowledgements

Thank you to my editor Alison Jack, as always, for her kind comments about the book and for suggestions, corrections and amendments that make it a more polished read.

Thanks to my beta readers for comments and suggestions, and for their time given to reading the early drafts.

Thanks to my immediate circle of friends who are so patient with me when I'm absorbed in my fictional world and for your continued support in all my endeavours.

I have to say thank you to my cruise loving friends for joining me on some of the most precious experiences of my life and to the cruise lines for making every holiday a special one.

Other Books by Dawn Brookes

Rachel Prince Mysteries

#1 A Cruise to Murder
#2 Deadly Cruise
#3 Killer Cruise
#4 Dying to Cruise

Memoirs

Hurry up Nurse: memoirs of nurse training in the 1970s
Hurry up Nurse 2: London calling

Coming Soon 2019

Book 5 in the *Rachel Prince Mystery* series
A Christmas Cruise Murder
Book 3 in the *Hurry up Nurse* series
Hurry up Nurse 3

Look out for new series
Carlos Jacobi PI

Picture Books for Children

Ava & Oliver's Bonfire Night Adventure
Ava & Oliver's Christmas Nativity
Adventure
Danny the Caterpillar
Gerry the One-Eared Cat

CPSIA information can be obtained
at www.ICGtesting.com
Printed in the USA
FSHW010811310821
84424FS